## Summer kissed his lips to steal a taste

Jackson possessed a full, soft mouth for a man of such chiseled features and hard angles. Her eyelids fell shut, heightening the sensations of his kiss. The warm whiskey taste of him intoxicated her, made her even bolder.

Splaying a hand across his broad chest beneath his jacket, she absorbed the feel of starched cotton and warm muscle through his white dress shirt. Her fingertips itched to cover more ground, to explore the terrain of the rock-hard abs currently plastered against her. To follow the silky path of his tie to the leather of his belt then and dip lower still....

He deepened their kiss, delving into her mouth to join them further. Summer closed her eyes more tightly against the onslaught of heat, the tingly wave of needy sensation that tripped through her whole body. As his tongue probed hers, an answering shock wave pulsed through her.

She had to have this man...*now.*

Dear Reader,

Have you ever met a guy in an unusual manner? Maybe accepted a date with someone you wouldn't have considered before, because his approach was just too standout to ignore? Jackson Taggart *really* wants to meet Summer Farnsworth in *Girl's Guide to Hunting & Kissing*, and he's not willing to trot out the stale old pick-up lines for an introduction. Would you say yes to a man who tried his tactics?

Welcome back to South Beach for the second book in my new series! Now that Brianne and Aidan have embarked on their happily-ever-after—*Sex & The Single Girl*, Blaze #104— ambiance coordinator Summer Farnsworth is starting to feel the tug of dissatisfaction with the lack of eligible men in her life. But can she date a guy who needs to play by the rules all the time? Of course, she might find it hard to resist a man as determined as Jackson to get what he wants.

If you enjoy *Girl's Guide to Hunting & Kissing*, I hope you'll join me for next month's SINGLE IN SOUTH BEACH story. *One Naughty Night* will be a November Temptation title, #951, and we'll finally get the scoop on Giselle Cesare's sexy older brother, Renzo. Visit me at www.JoanneRock.com to learn more about my future releases or to let me know what you think about the series so far!

Happy reading,

*Joanne Rock*

## Books by Joanne Rock

**HARLEQUIN BLAZE**
26—SILK, LACE & VIDEOTAPE
48—IN HOT PURSUIT
54—WILD AND WILLING
87—WILD AND WICKED
104—SEX & THE SINGLE GIRL*

**HARLEQUIN TEMPTATION**
863—LEARNING CURVES
897—TALL, DARK AND DARING
919—REVEALED

*Single in South Beach

# GIRL'S GUIDE TO HUNTING & KISSING

*Joanne Rock*

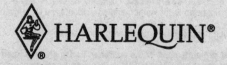

# HARLEQUIN®

TORONTO • NEW YORK • LONDON
AMSTERDAM • PARIS • SYDNEY • HAMBURG
STOCKHOLM • ATHENS • TOKYO • MILAN • MADRID
PRAGUE • WARSAW • BUDAPEST • AUCKLAND

For Michele Goes, my childhood friend who always encouraged me to tell stories with a happy ending. From our Barbie scenarios to our bedtime stories, we wanted the women to triumph! Thank you, Michele, for helping me to realize a dream. I wish you every happiness.

ISBN 0-373-79112-7

GIRL'S GUIDE TO HUNTING & KISSING

Copyright © 2003 by Joanne Rock.

Visit us at www.eHarlequin.com

**Printed in U.S.A.**

# 1

*Let the hunt begin…*

BREASTS BOUNCED in every direction on the dance floor of the Moulin Rouge Lounge. The hottest new nightclub on South Beach overflowed with women dressed in clothes that would be at home on the beach as much as the bar scene—halter tops, plunging necklines and enough Lycra to clothe the U.S. swim team well into the next decade.

Despite the dazzling display of feminine flesh highlighted by flashing blue strobe lights, attorney Jackson Taggart wasn't looking for breasts. Other guys might get caught up in cup sizes or long legs, but for his first venture into Miami's decadent nightlife in nearly a year, Jackson narrowed his focus to one thing.

Tonight, he'd sell his soul for the woman with the right…mouth.

In an effort to forget the hell his private life had become over the last few weeks, he watched women of every shape and size flirt, dance and sip brightly colored drinks from the Moulin Rouge's signature bar glasses featuring the frilly panties of a cancan girl with long, stocking clad legs.

He had a certain woman in mind, a woman unlike any he'd ever been with before. A bedroom goddess who didn't give a damn about his well-known family or the scandal of the decade in which they were currently ensnared.

Flagging a brunette bartender dressed in a uniform of silky white lingerie, Jackson started to request his standard imported beer and stopped himself. The hunt for a wild bedroom goddess at least deserved a shot of whiskey. His order given, he settled in for the search, eager to engage in anything that didn't involve damage control in the media, angry family shouting matches and an ever-looming pressure to enter a cutthroat state legislature race.

Damn.

Tossing back his whiskey, he concentrated on a single, simple task.

Finding the right mouth.

He scanned the crowd and found…pink bubblegum lips. Nah. Too sweet for what he had in mind. And even worse, too much like his ex-girlfriend.

Sparkly gold lips. High-maintenance diva—not a chance.

Bright-red lips looked wild enough, but broadening his visual scan he noted that the pale face and solid black outfit looked a bit Goth. Too moody.

None of those mouths pointed to the kind of woman he needed to find. But he had no intention of going home unfulfilled. Not this time.

Then he spied them.

The deep, rich muted burgundy that was neither too red nor too purple. Soft, full lips that suggested lush sensuality. A lack of shiny lip gloss made for a mouth that was at once kissable and not too self-conscious.

Bingo.

Jackson flung a bill across the bar to pay for his drink, scarcely noticing the glass-encased waterfall behind the throng of busy bartenders. Already on the move, he followed the woman who had caught his attention as she turned away and headed toward the back of the room.

From the brief glimpse he'd snagged of her face, he acknowledged she was uncommonly pretty. Still, he had a vague impression of her being a little unusual. Something about the odd mix of fabrics in her rosy-hued dress with the ragged hem maybe, or the wavy flaxen mermaid hair decorated with scattered thin braids that looked to be...pink?

He caught up with her just inside the bar's back room—a decadent lounge ringed with private, curtained booths. She met a tall woman with auburn hair and kick-ass legs dressed in an unadorned, steel-gray cat suit. He didn't bother checking out her lips. He'd already found perfection.

Straying closer to their position near a scaled-down minibar, Jackson didn't necessarily mean to overhear them. They shouted over the music, making it nearly impossible not to hear them. Especially considering he loomed just a few feet away.

"No luck with the manhunt?" the auburn-haired woman asked between sips of a green drink. Margarita, maybe.

The blonde shook her head and rolled her eyes. She was as expressive as the redhead was reserved. "Every guy I've met here has been too forward, too obvious and too eager to cut to the chase. I'm not asking for big-time romance, Bri. I'd just like to see a little originality in the approach. I mean, where's the..."

The sudden whirr of a blender at the minibar drowned out the rest. Jackson leaned forward, more than a little curious to know what the woman with the world's most perfect lips had to say about her personal turn-ons. But by the time the blender switched off, the redhead spoke.

"...then again, Aidan is pretty much a case study in originality."

The name caught his attention and made a few mental wheels turn. Jackson's friend and former college roommate, federal agent Aidan Maddock had just got engaged to one of the new part owners of Club Paradise.

Could it be the same woman?

While he puzzled that out, the blonde yanked her friend by the arm. "Come on. You've got to come see my latest little pleasure palace. You're going to love it."

Pleasure palace?

Jackson could have used another drink—or two— as he contemplated what exactly these gorgeous females had in mind. Obviously women were discussing things a hell of a lot more interesting than the status of the NASDAQ and baseball box scores when they hit the bars.

Determined to keep those lips in his sights, he followed the pair as they leaned close to one another, whispering and laughing as they edged through the crowd.

Damn.

Picking up speed, he tracked them out the back doors of the club leading to the exclusive resort connected to the Moulin Rouge Lounge and followed them past the semierotic paintings gracing the spacious corridors.

Careful to stay well behind the women, Jackson watched the blonde flounce down the hallway, a definite swing to her hips.

"It has tons of erotic potential," the bedroom goddess confided to her friend as she straightened some kind of see-through red shawl flung around her shoulders. "Not that I'll ever be able to make use of it, but I'm sure other people will benefit from my ingenuity."

"No whips and chains, I hope?" The tall redhead checked the oversize watch on her wrist while Jackson gulped.

"Now Brianne, you know we only allow velvet shackles. But this is much more refined. Very hot, very red. The room practically oozes sex."

They rounded a corner and Jackson couldn't possibly turn back. More than ever, he wanted to taste the lips of a woman who saw erotic potential and oozing sex in something so mundane as a room. How much pleasure might a woman like that find in a man?

The prospect effectively drowned out ninety percent of the other concerns that had been dogging his heels for the last month. Tonight he would pursue what *he* wanted instead of what everyone else expected from him.

While he wasn't exactly Mr. Uptight, he'd never been a player, either. He'd always dated women from the right social circles with ambitions similar to his own. Ordinarily, he never played games.

And he'd never sought a woman purely for the sake of sex.

But the blonde had him curious. He just needed to

find a way to meet her that was...what had she said she wanted?...original. And not too forward.

Hell, his ambitious clan had raised him to be politically correct in every facet of his life, how hard could it be to come up with something that wasn't too forward?

Ducking behind a vending machine as the women turned down yet another hallway, Jackson peered out just enough to see his prey shove a tall housekeeping supply cart into the doorway of a guest room and then slip inside.

Pretty damned convenient she'd left the door propped open.

Growing more certain that he'd found the right woman, Jackson strategized the best approach.

What would it hurt if—just this once—he applied all that smooth-talking charm that made the Taggarts famous for something besides courtroom closing arguments or speeches in the latest election race?

If he had his way, he'd be sweet-talking the blonde into helping him forget the nonstop disaster his life had become. At least for the next few hours, but even better, the next few days. With any luck, he'd find the wild bedroom goddess of his dreams.

He stepped lightly down the hallway toward the open guest-room door. Peering around the housekeeping cart piled high with guest towels, soaps and tissue boxes to get another glimpse of the unusual beauty, he discovered what she'd meant by a pleasure palace.

Damned if she hadn't walked into the silky red luxury of a modern-day bordello.

SUMMER FARNSWORTH turned up the lights in the Bad Girl Bordello and looked around at her latest creation.

"Oh my God, Summer, it's amazing." Club Paradise's security expert Brianne Wolcott sank into the room, her feet drawn to the red quilted settee outlined in cherrywood. "A visual feast."

"It still gives me shivers to walk in here." Preening openly, Summer soaked up her friend's praise. As part owner and a self-described ambiance coordinator for the club, she took her job seriously. She'd worked as an activities director for the club during the previous ownership. The gig had been awarded to her by a snake-in-the-grass ex-boyfriend who'd absconded with all the resort's profits.

Club Paradise had done a booming business as a couples resort for years before the major shareholders had embezzled the company's money. Since then, the women who'd been left behind by the crooks—an ex-wife, two ex-girlfriends and, in Brianne's case, a stepdaughter—had formed a new holding company. Admittedly cynical about love in the aftermath of the Rat Pack's defection, the new owners had converted the former couples haven into a hedonistic playground for singles.

Of course, Brianne wasn't so cynical about love anymore. She and hottie Aidan Maddock had found happiness—and, it seemed, plenty of sexual contentment—over the last two months. Her friend's fulfillment left Summer feeling all the more restless recently.

"Just be careful," Summer warned as Brianne ran her fingers over the fresh varnish. "The finish is still tacky in some places. The fumes aren't quite as bad since the afternoon, but it helps to leave the door open anyway for some fresh air.''

Glancing toward the propped door, Summer stared into the empty hallway behind her, unable to shake the feeling that someone had been there. Watching.

Normally, she possessed a finely tuned sixth sense. She knew when her parents were in trouble with whatever cult of the month they happened to have joined. She could tell when she was being lied to. And she could usually feel eyes on her from fifty paces, but apparently that particular skill was on the fritz tonight.

Although her skin prickled along the back of her neck and her heart skipped along at a nervous rate, no sexy stranger lurked in the doorway waiting to pounce.

Too bad.

Tearing her eyes from the hallway, she wondered if the last year's worth of stifled sexual impulses could account for her hallucinating a stranger on her tail. Or maybe she could attribute the fanciful thoughts to being in the Bad Girl Bordello.

''This room is definitely naughty.'' Brianne's voice called her back to the present. She trailed appreciative fingers over the lush shirred velvet lining two of the walls. ''Total fantasy.''

The deep burgundy color of the fabric was repeated in the bed and on an old-fashioned settee. Red satin trimmed with black lace skirted the bed and decorated pillows. Beaded antique lampshades rested over delicate brass light fixtures, while small crystal chandeliers twinkled in the soft light overhead.

''Told you it was a pleasure palace.'' Summer reached to tweak one of the dangling prisms in the chandelier near the entry.

As in several other rooms throughout the hotel, the bordello featured erotic statues and framed lithographs of a couple in various positions described in the *Kama Sutra*. Even so, the room had taken on a mood and ambiance uniquely its own.

"Yes, but will you christen this room as thoroughly as Aidan and I christened the harem?" Brianne winked as she started rifling through the bags of thematic costumes Summer had bought as amenities for the luxury suite.

A rogue twinge of envy squeezed Summer as she thought about the kinds of pleasures Brianne and her new fiancé Aidan Maddock had enjoyed at the club. They'd been the first couple to make use of the sensual atmosphere Summer strove to maintain in all the refurbished rooms.

"Actually, I'm hoping to snag this room any time it's free, but we'll probably have lots of reservations for it once a few people have stayed here." Summer had lived at the hotel for the last year, bouncing from room to room according to whatever was available. "I seem to be short a man for any real christening, but I have to say if I had an opportunity, this room would be my first choice."

Some optimistic part of her had hoped to initiate a real relationship at this stage of her life. At twenty-eight years old, she was the only female she knew in her age bracket who had never formed a remotely long-term liaison.

Of course, that desire for a mild commitment had prevented her from making moves on the guys she'd always been most attracted to—the surfers with the rebel attitudes and the rock 'n' roll studs who were living on the edge. Somehow she couldn't work up the same lusty enthusiasm for the more staid investment brokers, entrepreneurs and lawyerly types that invaded South Beach nightlife.

"Want me to start keeping an eye out for you, Summer? I think I know your type. Unconventional, lives-by-his-own rules kind of guy, right?" Brianne pulled a crushed silk corset out of Summer's costume bag and grazed the fabric against her cheek.

Summer frowned, surprised. "Since when did you become the intuitive one, Ms. High Tech?"

"You're parading around the club wearing a vintage bustier and pink braids in your hair. Believe me, pure logic brought me to the conclusion you'd like an unconventional guy."

"A bustier this gorgeous needed to be seen." Shaking off the crocheted scarf she'd draped over her shoulders, Summer unveiled the silk moiré undergarment she'd snagged for herself during the costume-shopping spree.

She could have sworn she heard a swift intake of breath in the corridor outside the door.

What was it with her and the damn hallway tonight? The sense of someone watching her lingered. But she knew perfectly well Brianne had taken the extra remote security cameras out of the private rooms. No doubt the hot gaze she felt merely resulted from a shivery manifestation of overactive hormones.

Brianne tugged one of Summer's decorative pink braids. "I think you've crossed over into the fantasy world you created. Did you realize your bustier coordinates perfectly with the bordello?"

"You think *this* is fantasy?" Summer adjusted the

satin ribbon tying her outfit together. "This doesn't come close to the ideas I have in mind if I ever found the right guy to christen the bordello with."

Brianne pulled the requisite velvet shackles out of Summer's costume bag and dangled them in front of her nose. "Would you make him your love slave?"

"Hardly."

"You don't have kinky toe fetishes or anything, do you?"

"Eeeww." Summer whipped Brianne's shoulder with one end of her satin bustier tie. "I'm thinking more along the lines of being totally overwhelmed." She gestured vaguely around the room. "That's sort of the whole bordello theme in a nutshell, isn't it—being at a man's whim? I mean don't get me wrong, obviously we're all grateful the women's movement has given us so much power over our lives, but sometimes I feel ready to shake off the *überwoman* syndrome and just be…"

"*Over*powered?" Brianne fanned herself. "Honey, that's a smoking fantasy. Where do I sign up for that?"

"It's definitely not on Club Paradise's activity list. If it was, I'd be the first to sign on." She could certainly use the stress-relieving benefits of sex. She'd been giving one hundred and ten percent to the hotel in an effort to prepare the rooms for a possible print pictorial in *Wanderlust* magazine this fall. The spread would be a professional coup, but it would mean publicly staking her success—and the resort's—on her design talent.

Summer peered toward the door again, her skin tingling along with that overactive sixth sense.

Or maybe her skin simply tingled from thinking about her favorite seduction scenario.

"I'm right there with you." Brianne stood, her eyes now glued on the miniature surveillance monitor she'd installed in a sort of wristwatch contraption. "But for now I'd better go check the security and make sure things are running smoothly around the club tonight."

With a few more exclamations over the bordello, Brianne was out the door, leaving Summer by herself to unload the exotic lingerie costumes into a decorative armoire.

She turned back to the task, hanging corsets and merry widows from quilted pink hangers in the cherry cabinet.

Yet the maddening sensation of being watched returned. Spinning around, she followed her instincts this time, unconcerned if she was being paranoid. She skirted the settee and hustled to the open door. Leaning over the housekeeping supply cart, she poked her head out into the corridor and saw nothing. No one.

Brianne had disappeared in the hallway and no one else lurked there.

Okay, so she was definitely paranoid. Easing back into the bordello, Summer edged around the housekeeping cart. The satin ties on her bustier trailed over a stack of fresh towels and a shiny silver box.

No. A cell phone.

She reached for the item. As her fingers grazed the cool metal it started to vibrate.

A shivery sensation skated through her for a split second, confirming that she'd denied her sexual impulses for too long.

Jiggling the stack of cotton towels beneath it, the

phone hummed and then emitted a shrill ring. Never a woman to mind her own business, Summer unfolded the sleek case and willed away the stray tingles humming through her.

"Hello?" She tucked back into the bordello, hugging the phone to her ear with one shoulder.

"Thanks for picking up." A smooth and sexy masculine voice rolled through the airwaves. "I'm trying to track down my cell phone so I thought I'd ring the number and see what happened."

He'd ignited a lonely woman's libido with a vibrating phone. How perfectly clever.

"You seem to have misplaced it on a housekeeping cart." She glanced back at the maid's apparatus and wondered what the man on the other end of this amazing voice might look like. "Right between the triple-milled French soaps and the lavender hand lotions."

"Of all the places to land in an exotic hotel, I get stuck in the rolling soap-supply station."

"Actually, the soap station was teetering on the threshold of the Bad Girl Bordello. I call that kind of exotic." A smile warmed her insides. When was the last time she'd flirted with a man?

"Now that sounds more like it. I don't know how my phone ended up there, but I did wander through the resort earlier tonight before I went into the bar. I'm Jackson, by the way. Would you mind if I came by to pick up the phone?"

Mentally she reviewed why that wouldn't be a good idea. She should meet him in a public place like the lounge just in case he was a serial killer. Then again, she could always just ask Brianne to check on her in a little while.

"Sure. I'm Summer Farnsworth and the phone will be with me in the bordello." Could she help it if her inner bad girl still made occasional appearances? "It's on the ocean side of the main floor."

"I'm on my way." The line disconnected as she folded up the phone.

Hesitating a moment, she opened it again and placed a quick call to Brianne to make sure her friend would keep an eye out for her tonight. Brianne's experience with a creepy stalker had made everyone at Club Paradise a little more cautious.

That done, Summer was feeling less paranoid by the moment. In fact, she felt downright eager. She suspected she was about to meet the man behind the eyes she'd sensed on her this evening. Her every intuitive Aquarian impulse told her so. Instead of frightening her, however, the thought only heightened her anticipation.

This guy—Jackson—had gone out of his way to hunt her down and meet her. He'd used a very non-traditional means that could turn a girl's head. Maybe he was the kind of sexy rebel that had always attracted her. And while she had tried to outgrow the flings of her youth, she couldn't deny a hot, quickie interlude with a mysterious stranger might be just the cure for her recent restlessness.

As she dug in her vintage beaded handbag for a tube of lipstick, Summer made up her mind to jump her visitor if he had a tattoo. She'd jump him twice if he had a tattoo *and* an earring.

Which left her with only one thing to ponder.

Would tonight's Mistress of the Bordello leave her bustier ties opened or closed?

# 2

---

*While stalking your prey, be sure to dress for the kill.*

JACKSON STRAIGHTENED his tie outside the doorway labeled Bordello on a creamy slab of light-colored marble. The maid's cart still propped the door open, so he hung back a moment to gather his thoughts while a sultry blues tune drifted through the open archway into the hall. He began to button his suit jacket and then, on second thought, left the olive gabardine garment undone.

If Summer proved to be half as flirtatious in person as she'd been over the phone, maybe he wouldn't be leaving his jacket on for long anyway. A woman who designed sexy bordellos for a living couldn't be all that reserved.

Besides, he possessed privileged information to give him an edge in his seduction quest.

He knew Summer's secret fantasy.

Not that he planned to use the information—yet. His knuckle hovered over the door as he debated tonight's approach. When she'd given him her name over the phone, he'd identified her as one of the four primary owners of the revamped club. Translation—she was hip-deep in scandal and controversy herself these days. Many Miami Beach residents had been cheated out of their investments with the club's former owners and they didn't necessarily approve of the business's reorganization and reopening.

Just what a politician needed—to be linked to someone making all the wrong headlines.

Still, he wanted Summer. Badly. And he couldn't officially call himself a politician yet. Despite pressure on all sides, Jackson hadn't thrown his hat in the ring for state legislator in his district.

Reaching around the housekeeping cart to rap on the bordello door with a bit more force than he'd intended, Jackson made up his mind to live for himself tonight. He'd been a prisoner to the press and his family's high-profile lifestyle too damn long.

He waited, watching the propped door swing all the way open while Billie Holiday belted out a torch song within.

Summer Farnsworth and her bedroom goddess mouth were there—utterly delectable and framed in a backdrop of crimson. Her ruby-red dress blended with the rest of the room while her creamy pale skin and platinum-blond hair stood out all the more. Shoulders bared in a tiny top that had to be some sort of undergarment, she had untied the ribbon that laced the outfit together.

Could she be thinking along the same seductive lines as him tonight?

His gaze searched her face for those answers, but she seemed to be studying him with every bit as much fascination. Her eyes lingered on his tie.

He could have sworn she mumbled something about no tattoo under her breath, but obviously he'd misheard.

She glanced up at him while she refastened the loosened ties just above her breasts.

Damn.

"You're Jackson Taggart." Her lips cocked in a wry grin not exactly brimming with enthusiasm. Tiny crescent moons dangled from her ears.

"Didn't I mention that on the phone?" Of course he knew damn well he hadn't. His family name carried all the wrong connotations in the press lately.

"You just said Jackson. I would have remembered the Taggart part." Still, she stepped aside and gestured him in. "Let me get your phone."

Not wanting to push his luck, he stood just inside the doorway and waited while she crossed the room to a sitting area. He watched with appreciative eyes as she edged her way around the antique furniture, her gently swaying hips inviting attention.

She bent to retrieve his phone from a table covered with silky black satin and lace. Good God, the woman had buried his phone in lingerie.

Knowing he was going to be shown the door in about two seconds if he let this silence stretch out any further, he tore his eyes from Summer and her undergarments with an effort. "I have to admit, I was pretty curious what a bordello looked like. Thanks for letting me in."

Cradling the phone in her palm, she tapped the antenna against her chin in a rhythmic motion. "I'm banking on your very public reputation that you're a gentleman. Just in case, I told my girlfriend to make periodic drive-bys to make sure I'm safe in here. If she doesn't hear from me at the designated time…"

She shrugged, leading him to believe he'd be a dead man with the bodyguard.

Still, he had to admit it was a clever plan. "Good thinking." But he had no intention of cruising forward too fast and possibly overstepping his welcome. "Being in the public eye definitely gives me a high level of accountability for my actions."

And, lately, his father's actions.

She wandered closer, still toying with his phone. "So you need to color inside the lines in your type of work, Jackson?"

His name on her lips slid over him like the silky blues music—sweet and seductive. "Can't hurt to play it safe when you know your actions will only be dissected in the morning news."

Pausing a few feet in front of him, she extended her hand and the cell phone she carried. "And yet you followed me tonight."

Mesmerized by the way her mouth curled around her words as she spoke, Jackson almost missed their meaning. "What?"

"You weren't exactly coloring inside the lines when you followed me and Brianne to the bordello earlier." Her gray eyes pinned him, measuring him.

Suddenly his tie felt way too damn tight.

"You knew?" So much for smooth-talking his way into meeting her. He obviously wasn't nearly as slick as he'd thought.

Waiting for her to boot him out into the hallway, he took the phone she still held out to him. His fingers brushed hers, sending a current of pure sensation through his hand.

"I'm very intuitive." She shrugged and the dangling crescent moons in her ears grazed her shoulders. "Highly developed sixth sense. Want me to guess what you're thinking right now?"

He was thinking how fast he'd blown his chance of ever being naked with this woman. "I'm rather hoping you won't guess, actually. And I'm sorry about following you. It certainly hadn't been my intent to make you uncomfortable."

"No?" She smiled as if thoroughly enjoying herself.

Jackson was now totally out of his element. "I only hoped to meet you, but you left the lounge before I had the chance."

"So you put your phone on the housekeeping cart on purpose?" She studied him so hard Jackson wondered if she was attempting to read his thoughts again.

Just in case, he concentrated on thinking about what a good guy he could be. Normally.

"I wanted to find a way to meet you that wouldn't make me look like Joe Stalker." He backed up a step toward the door, knowing he sounded like a lunatic. Good thing he hadn't told her he'd been lured to follow her by her lips. "I'll understand if you want me to take off now."

Even though he'd hate it.

He wanted this outrageous woman more than he wanted his next breath. And no matter what he told her, Jackson didn't have any intention of backing off all together. She might look at him and draw conclusions about him from the suit, but she had no way of knowing the restless man inside it.

The restless, determined-as-hell man inside it.

He hadn't won a reputation in the courtroom by

trotting out generations of Taggart good breeding and polite manners. No, he'd earned a win-loss record any prizefighter would envy by single-minded pursuit of his goals.

And somehow over the course of this evening, Summer Farnsworth had become a goal he damn well planned to attain.

SUMMER HAD ALWAYS been able to size up people.

As a child, she'd known when her parents had chosen a good cult to get involved with and when they'd landed in a militant crowd that would make all their lives a living hell.

Right now, her sixth sense told her she could trust Jackson Taggart—even if he seemed to be thinking some deep thoughts right now as he stared back at her. He might have used underhanded means to meet her, but she had to give him points for originality. In fact, she was damned flattered he'd gone to so much trouble not to spook her.

At six-foot-plus, he dwarfed her by a good five inches. His neatly buzzed sandy hair was bleached blond at the tips, attesting to a Floridian love of the sun. A strong jaw, cheekbones she would kill for and steely blue eyes made him a gorgeous man.

It was the suit that had thrown her.

Crisply pressed and perfectly pleated, his olive suit looked expensive, high-class, and just a little too starchy for her tastes. Not that she'd ever been quick to judge a book by its cover, but something about his slick exterior made her think he wouldn't appreciate a woman who wore a bustier in public.

Then again, he might not be the tattoo-bearing, earring-wearing superstud she'd been hoping to meet, but the beach-bum muscle-heads she used to date hadn't exactly provided lasting fulfillment.

Jackson Taggart was considered one of Miami Beach's hottest bachelors, and he certainly filled out his suit in all the right places.

Maybe she just needed to get to know him a little better before making any decisions. If he turned out to be a stuffy, no-fun politician type, she would be able to walk away from him easily. But after their intriguing meeting, she could at least find out more about him.

"You don't have to go." She nodded toward the intimate sitting area on the other side of the room. "Why don't you have a seat and tell me about your political ambitions instead?"

The smile he shot her sent a shimmer of tingly heat through her. The man would win any election with a grin like that.

"You're going to make me accountable for my actions now, too, aren't you?" He extended his hand in the classic "after you" gesture.

Had she ever dated a man who'd done the "after you" thing?

She obliged him, making her way to the newly varnished settee so he could have the safer seating of a taupey-gold colored wingback. Only, Jackson didn't take a seat. He prowled about the bordello, about her, at a leisurely pace.

Summer watched him for a moment as he lightly fingered the shirred-velvet walls, exploring their lush softness.

Clearing her throat to cover the sudden catch in her

breath, Summer chose to ignore his wandering fingers and answer his question.

"I just figured since you tricked me into this meeting, the least you can do is let me in on the truth behind all the Miami Beach gossip. Is it true you're going to make a late election bid for state legislator?"

"You follow politics?" He glanced her way as he moved on toward the cherry armoire. Slowly. Deliberately.

She had a momentary vision of him in the courtroom, stalking the witnesses on the stand with his deceptively casual stroll.

"Not usually. But it just so happens your photo ends up in the paper on all the same days mine does so I've been sort of following the rumors surrounding you." The media continually questioned his integrity when, in fact, it obviously had been his father who'd screwed up by accepting kickbacks from criminals in his long-ago position as an FBI director.

Still, the local paper had been quick to put Jackson under a microscope, scrutinizing every facet of his personal and professional life. Which, now that she thought about it, was a definite strike against getting involved with this man. Summer's funky clothes and penchant for wearing crystals to resonate with whatever energies she happened to need in her life at the moment would never bear up well under a microscope.

Especially not when her mood crystals were paired with a straight-laced politician.

"They're not true." At the moment, he had walked somewhere behind her, so she couldn't gauge his expression. Instead, his voice rumbled through her from a few feet away, the low, quiet intensity of his words giving passion to the statement. "I'm trying to understand my father's decisions but that doesn't mean I'm doomed to make the same ones."

He seemed to loom closer as he spoke. Summer's neck tingled all over again with that sensation of being watched. Studied. Assessed.

Goose bumps rose on her arms, the sensation not entirely unpleasant. She fought to stay focused on their words instead of the peculiar physical dance taking place in the room. That chatty sixth sense of hers told her she was way out of her depth with this man.

Curving her hands about her shoulders to warm the chill bumps away, Summer considered Jackson's tenuous position in the public eye.

"Believe me, I wouldn't want to be judged by my parents' actions." She adored Willow and Phoenix Farnsworth, but their lifestyle was far from normal. "I don't know how you handle so much inquiry into your business."

She'd hated that about the cults her parents had continually joined. There were too many bizarre rules, too much close contact with people who wanted to regulate your life. No, thank you. She would not "regulate" anything about herself again. Ever.

Jackson shifted behind her. Moving closer?

She waited, wondered what he might be doing back there until the soft fabric of the crocheted shawl she'd worn earlier fell around her goose-bump-covered shoulders. Out of the corner of her eye, she spied Jackson's hands on the garment for a fraction of a second before he released it, those long tanned fingers nearly grazing the back of the settee. Nearly grazing *her*. She sensed the heat of his body, could almost guess what those hands would feel like on her.

And instead of chasing away a chill, her shawl only increased the cool quiver dancing along her skin.

Tugging the ends of the shawl a little closer to wrap around her midsection, Summer watched as Jackson resumed his lazy prowl around the room.

As if he hadn't just sent a shock wave of latent desire through her system.

He toyed with a framed photo on the writing desk, a gilt frame that she knew perfectly well contained turn-of-the-century erotica in the form of a naked woman playing piano.

"I remember going to my first press conference riding on my dad's shoulders. I guess it hasn't bothered me in the past because I was used to it. It's getting a little too intense for me now, though." His gaze traveled from the photo to her. He studied her with those magnetic blue eyes, his relaxed posture totally at odds with the heat of that steady gaze. "I came to the club tonight to take my mind off the whole mess. The pressure has been...distracting."

Summer shifted in her seat, too aware of this man. The bustier that had felt so sexy an hour ago, now seemed to constrain her, provide too much friction against her breasts.

In an effort to get her mind off her rising temperature, she redirected their conversation. "You know, you never answered my question about the legislature bid."

"You don't miss a trick, do you?" He gave her a wicked grin before his attention shifted to the monstrous red-shrouded bed in the back of the room. "I couldn't answer you on that because I honestly haven't made up my mind yet."

Could he be serious? "No one joins an election in September."

His shrug wrinkled the perfect lines of his suit. Summer idly wondered what he would look like if she wrestled him to that big bed and messed up the rest of his tailored outfit. The Mistress of the Bordello would never let a man walk away without tousling him a bit, would she?

"Confidence is a good thing in my business, Summer." He eyed her as he smoothed a hand over the red satin duvet covering the mattress. And while she knew technically they were discussing politics, she had the distinct impression Jackson's confidence extended to the bedroom, as well.

No way could she delude herself that the man was the dry, buttoned-up type anymore. As of right now, she was toast where he was concerned. She wanted her one night with him. Badly.

While she debated how to make that one night a reality, Jackson blithely went back to discussing politics.

"Besides, I've got a solid track record in smaller elections. I've never lost yet." His gaze strayed to the pile of lingerie on the coffee table. "Is it going to be my turn to ask the questions any time soon?"

She smiled at that even as she wondered if confidence might be an aphrodisiac. If anyone else had boasted about never losing, Summer would have written it off as conceit. Yet Jackson seemed to be just relating facts, quietly sure of his ability.

And she had to admit, there was something damn

attractive about that. Not that she necessarily wanted to be turned on by a man so intrinsically wrong for her. She lived to create scandal while he worked diligently to avoid it.

Still, she couldn't deny she wanted him.

Would it hurt to follow this attraction for just one night? How much trouble could one night cause to a girl's heart?

"Can I ask you one more nosy question and then I'll let you off the hook?"

"Ask away." Tearing his gaze from the lingerie pile, he quirked a sandy eyebrow, waiting.

She picked at the ragged hem of her silky handkerchief skirt, certain he wouldn't be waiting patiently much longer. Her every feminine instinct told her he was ready to make a move, no matter how lazily he strolled the room right now.

Soon, Summer would be enjoying that supreme male confidence of his in a much more physical way. She glanced up at him through her lashes, hoping she had her seductive moves in place. "How exactly did you plan to blow off steam tonight?"

Jackson couldn't remember any pointed press conference question that had put him more on the spot than this one. His glance tripped over her willowy form draped across the settee, his eyes lingering on the satin ties that she'd refastened on her strapless crimson top.

By the time he managed to meet Summer's not-so-innocent gray gaze he decided he owed her the truth, even while he extended their cat-and-mouse game a little longer.

"After two weeks of mental turmoil, I wanted to

escape to a realm of pure physical sensation. Blaring music, flashing lights, a shot of straight whiskey—anything that might drown out the rest of the world for a little while.''

''I think you're forgetting one very obvious physical sensation that South Beach nightlife often provides.'' She retrieved the satin ties that lay across her arm and absently wound one end around her finger.

He caught the invitation behind the words. And he'd bet many a man would have made a dive for her right then and there.

But despite Summer's come-hither outfit and the wild pink braids in her blond mermaid hair, Jackson guessed there were more layers to this woman than the sexy veneer. Her knowledgeable questions about his work had surprised him. Pleasantly so. And she couldn't be the seduction queen her outfit implied if she was still sitting politely on her antique settee after he'd been in this pleasure palace of hers for nearly an hour.

If he leaped at his first chance with her, he might find one night of incredible physical sensation. And granted, that's what he'd thought he wanted when he'd walked into Club Paradise tonight—pleasure without commitment.

Their conversation had made him rethink the strategy. Her scandal-making, adventurous nature fascinated him, appealed to his own wild side that he'd kept under wraps by necessity because of his family. His job.

But hell, his old man had basically incinerated the family name so he didn't need to worry about that anymore. And as for his job, maybe he wouldn't even have a shot at the election given the scandal surrounding him.

It seemed he was suffering all the effects of negative press and he hadn't had any of the fun of creating it.

Maybe he wanted something more from Summer Farnsworth than a night of incredible sex. He didn't know what that might be, but he had the feeling he would never have the chance to find out if he rushed headlong into a physical relationship.

He studied her now while Ella Fitzgerald sang, could see the surprise in her eyes that he hadn't made a move on her yet. The curiosity.

He moved closer to her. Sank into the chair she'd pointed out to him earlier. Leaning forward to prop his elbows on his knees, Jackson wanted to make it clear that just because he didn't jump her right away didn't mean he wasn't interested. "The prospect of sex definitely entered my mind when I walked into the club tonight."

"How about when you walked into the bordello?" Summer shifted her legs, re-crossing them in the other direction and giving him plenty of opportunity to glimpse toned calves and a hint of creamy thighs below the jagged hem of her skirt.

Delayed gratification wasn't going to be a stroll in the park when it came to this woman. But he had goals to achieve, damn it. He didn't have any intention of wavering from his chosen path.

"What was I thinking when a gorgeous woman ushered me into a red velvet bordello and conversed with me over a pile of exotic lingerie?" He flicked an errant bra strap sliding off the edge of the coffee table. "I'll bet you have a good idea what I'm thinking. That doesn't mean I'm going to act on it.''

He nearly changed his mind when he saw a flash of disappointment—quickly concealed—in her light-gray eyes.

She released the red satin ties to her outfit she'd been playing with and tugged her shawl more tightly around her shoulders. ''How...noble of you.''

''Not noble. Just patient. Ten seconds into our conversation tonight I realized I wanted to know you better than any night of rushed sex would ever allow.'' As he spoke the words, he embraced the objective all the more. There was something very intriguing about this woman who dressed like a gypsy, flirted with a vengeance and owned a quarter of the hottest new spot on South Beach. Not the least of which was the fantasy he'd heard her relate to her girlfriend about being overpowered. What might it be like to play out that particular scenario with her? ''I'd rather not miss out on the chance to get to know you by fast-forwarding through the preliminaries.''

Relinquishing the garment she'd been clutching about herself, her jaw dropped for a split second before she snapped it shut again. ''You're not looking for sex. You just came into the bordello to talk?''

She spelled it all out as if to be certain of the facts. Damn. Was his request so unusual? And if it was, didn't that say something pretty freaking sorry about the condition of the dating scene in the new millennium?

''Honestly, sex would be very welcome at some point down the road.'' He concentrated on making eye contact with her so his gaze didn't unwittingly roam her tempting body. "I just hoped we could go out sometime."

"You and me?" Her tone told him she thought the idea ludicrous. She shook her head. "You'll never stop making scandalous headlines if you hit the town with me, Jackson. My clothes alone draw enough attention to keep me in the paper every week. Can you imagine what kind of press you'll get if I'm out on the town with South Beach's most beloved bachelor? You'll never win your election."

"Isn't that for me to worry about? And why should my personal life have to revolve around elections?" He'd been walking the straight and narrow for too damn long and for some reason it took meeting Summer with her bedroom goddess lips and decadent bordello to make him realize it.

She rose, brow furrowed, and edged around the coffee table to circle the sitting area. From the way her teeth sank into the soft fullness of her lower lip, Jackson gathered she was thinking. Worrying, maybe?

Pausing beside an open armoire, she folded her arms under small but oh-so-enticing breasts. "You're asking me on a date?"

"Are you already seeing someone?"

"No. But look at us." She gestured between her body and his. "Anyone could tell we're mismatched." She shook her head and started pacing again. "What sign are you?"

"What sign?"

Stopping again, she leaned against a sleek, unobtrusive marble wet bar and sighed. "When's your birthday?"

He had *so* lost the thread of this conversation. "May twelfth?"

"Of course, you're a Taurus. I'm an Aquarius." She withdrew a silver pendant that had been hidden under her dress. From his vantage point, it looked like a disk with a few wavy lines carved across the front. "You're the bull and I'm the ever-changing water sign. It will never work."

Ah. A challenge.

If Summer Farnsworth had known him better, she would have realized she couldn't chase him off by declaring he couldn't possibly win. Throughout the course of his career, challenges had always fueled him. Fired him up. Made him all the more determined.

Rising, he stepped closer to Summer. Plainly, the time had arrived to employ stronger means of persuasion. "This Aquarius condition…does that make you clairvoyant or something?"

She tilted her chin as he neared and he could almost see her dig her heels into the plush taupe carpet. "I once accurately predicted a hurricane in a Tarot-card reading. But in general, no, I'm not psychic."

"Then you can't possibly know what might happen between us if we got together." He stopped a fraction of an inch inside her personal space, just close enough to catch the wild floral scent of her.

"It just seems unwise for a man in your position to court trouble." Her breath caught, a fact he noticed since his glance had somehow strayed to her chest.

Dragging his attention back to her wide gray eyes, he concentrated on listening to her words as opposed to her body language.

"Especially when we have so little in common." She cleared her throat, licked the rim of her lips.

Too bad Summer talked in very articulate body language. Jackson didn't have a prayer of ignoring it.

Or her.

Or what he'd wanted from the moment he'd first spied that rosy-colored mouth of hers.

"It seems even more unwise to pretend we don't feel what's going on right now." He reached for her, his fingers skimming her jaw while his thumb found the soft fullness of her lower lip.

She swayed slightly. Her eyelids fluttered but refused to fall.

"I'm the kind of person who craves freedom. I break rules all the time. Just for fun." Her voice held a note of warning, mild panic. "Didn't I tell you I was the original bad girl behind the Bad Girl Bordello?"

Jackson had no interest in being warned off. The temperature between them cranked up a few more degrees, giving him no choice but to pull her to him and mold her slender body to his.

"I don't see you breaking any rules tonight, Summer. If I'm going to be convinced you're such a bad girl, I think you're going to have to prove it."

# 3

*Be aware that kissing can lead you into dangerous territory.*

PROOF?

Summer had greeted the man with her bustier untied and now she was practically unraveling in his arms from just a touch, yet he required proof of her wild and wanton streak?

Well by God, she would gladly show him.

Stretching up on her toes, she brushed her lips over his the way she'd wanted to for the last hour. Sitting beside sexy Jackson Taggart in the lush sensuality of the bordello room had made her more than a little edgy. And since the kiss was simply an exercise in proving a point, she didn't bother to hold anything back.

She flicked her tongue across his lips to steal a taste. He possessed a full, soft mouth for a man of such chiseled features and hard angles. Her eyelids fell shut, heightening the sensations of his kiss. The warm whiskey taste of him intoxicated her, made her even bolder.

Splaying a hand across his broad chest beneath his jacket, she absorbed the feel of starched cotton and warm muscle through his white dress shirt. Her fingertips itched to cover more ground, to explore the terrain of the rock-hard abs currently plastered against her. To follow the silky path of his tie to the leather of his belt and then dip lower still...

Yet she contented herself with reaching to touch his face, to cradle his rough-hewn jaw and stroke the crisp hair at the back of his neck. His aftershave smelled clean and expensive, elusive enough to make her want to linger so she might catch the scent more strongly.

But then Jackson expelled a throaty growl of pure male hunger and tightened his grip. Arms banded around her, he locked her body against his, his formerly still hands now coming to life.

He deepened their kiss, delving into her mouth to mate and join them. Summer closed her eyes more tightly against the onslaught of heat, the tingly wave of needy sensation that tripped through her whole body. As his tongue probed hers, an answering shock wave pulsed between her legs.

In the recesses of her brain, she heard the bluesy piano of Duke Ellington somewhere in the background, but even the vivid reds of the bordello were fading to black when forced to compete with the magnetic draw of this man.

Jackson.

In her mind's eye, she could see no one and nothing else. The heel of his hand smoothed over her cheek while his long fingers combed through her hair. Her scalp prickled with warmth while her breasts tightened against his chest.

The silk moiré bustier that she'd retied now strained at the seams with her erratic breathing. She could already anticipate what it would feel like to peel off the stiff fabric and press herself intimately to Jackson's hard chest.

Bliss.

She wanted this man with an intensity that surpassed any longing she'd ever felt for a tattooed surfer. How had she ever thought Jackson was low-key or laid-back when he kissed with the exquisite finesse of the devil himself?

He backed her closer to the bed recessed in a private alcove of the larger room. Or perhaps she drew him toward the bed. It seemed their chemistry had exploded all of a sudden, leaving them both in the grip of a power that was hotter and more volatile than either of them.

Her thigh skimmed the red satin coverlet as the black lace grazed her ankle. The dull thud at the back of her leg barely fazed her, but it seemed to bring Jackson back to life.

He broke off their kiss, his eyes refocusing on their surroundings.

On her.

"That's not so bad in my book, Summer." His voice hit a smoky note, blending in with the gravelly blues singer emanating from the bedside radio.

She struggled to recall what they'd been discussing, or what his words had to do with climbing into bed right now and not getting out for the next forty-eight hours. "Hmm?"

His hands wandered over her bare shoulders. Apparently she'd lost her shawl again on the way to the bed. Now, the warm pad of his finger gently cruised the slope of her collarbone then dipped into the hollow at the base of her throat.

Wasn't Brianne supposed to be making a few security checks on her tonight? If Summer didn't get some help soon, she would surely burst into flame from Jackson's touch.

"I said that wasn't so bad." His voice rumbled in his chest even as his whispered the words.

Summer felt the words as much as she heard them.

"Damn straight it wasn't so bad," she whispered back, debating how difficult it would be to topple him down onto the bed with her. "In fact, that was downright fantastic."

The distinct sound of a smothered laugh drew her attention from the logistics of maneuvering a six-foot-plus man into bed. Her gaze landed on a mouth suppressing a smile.

"I meant that *you* aren't so bad, Summer. As in, maybe you're not quite the bad girl you think you are." He twined his fingers through hers.

Ah. She'd rather forgotten that conversation and her last-ditch effort to scare him off before his kiss had rocked her world. In the past, she'd chosen quick liaisons with no-commitment men who were willing to follow her lead. While those relationships hadn't been overly fulfilling, they'd at least taken the edge off her sensual longings and allowed her to pretend she was in control.

But Jackson had a way of taking charge that unsettled her even though her body was already responding.

"Maybe kissing wasn't such a great way of showing off my wild side." Or maybe underneath Jackson Taggart's oh-so-refined suit beat the heart of a tattooed thrill seeker.

Then again, maybe he was nothing like any guy

she'd ever been with and she was totally out of her depth.

"Or maybe you're just not giving me enough credit for being able to take whatever you dish out."

A little thrill of a different kind skipped through her. Not that she would let it sway her decision. "I'm sure *you* could handle it. I'm more concerned that your public won't be able to."

"Then again, maybe you're just scared to take a chance on me." He leaned closer to look her in the eye, the challenge simmering in his words. The man looked mighty at home framed in the background of shirred burgundy velvet that covered the walls of the sensuous bordello.

Damn. How could she be so transparent to this guy? She hadn't been accused of being scared of anything since—well, since she'd been old enough to armor herself with wild clothes and crystal talismans. Her mystical image combined with a few random outrageous acts had always made people keep their distance.

Until now. She sniffed, hoping she could regain lost ground. "Hardly."

"Prove it. Go boating with me tomorrow." He called her on the bluff.

She shouldn't be surprised. Jackson had skillfully outmaneuvered her from the moment he'd strolled into the bordello in his deceptively buttoned-up suit.

"Boating?" Could she help it if her ears perked up a bit? She'd decided to quit her gypsy lifestyle and hang out in southern Florida on a permanent basis just because of the beach.

"No better place to improve your outlook than

skimming over gulf waters. You Aquarian types ought to appreciate that.'' He tugged the leather thong around her neck, dislodging the silver pendant with the water markings of her astrological sign from the narrow valley of her cleavage.

Did he realize how the action teased her breasts?

She gazed up at him and found heat smoldering in his eyes. Of course he knew what it did to her.

Still, she had no clue how to conduct a real relationship, and Jackson didn't seem to be interested in a one-night conflagration. What man wasn't interested in easy sex? Not that she had a vast amount of experience in that particular arena, but growing up in communes had given her a lot of knowledge.

She had to admit, a man who could deny immediate sex for the sake of something more possessed an admirable amount of control. She couldn't help but wonder what kind of sexual prowess a man with so much control might possess.

Still…

No matter how intriguing that particular thought might be, Summer knew she couldn't give him what he wanted.

Even if she wanted to venture into real-relationship terrain, a public figure on the verge of a big career move was definitely not the right kind of guy to play trial and error with.

Her errors would be dissected on the six o'clock news.

''Come on, Summer.'' He whispered the words in her ear like a devil perched on her shoulder. ''You can't let a straight-laced attorney one-up you in the thrill-seeking department. You're risking your reputation as a wild woman.''

She had to smile. "Who'd have thought South Beach's golden boy would turn out to be such an instigator?''

"Can I take that as a yes?''

No. No. No. Definitely not.

"Yes, on one condition." Damn it, how had she blurted that out? She hadn't consciously made up her mind when the words were tumbling from her lips. But then, her impetuous nature had brought her as much good luck in life as bad. She owned a quarter of the controlling shares of Club Paradise thanks to following a whim.

As long as she kept an upper hand in this relationship, she would be okay. And her condition would provide that edge she needed to stay in charge.

"Name it.''

Reaching up to his neck, she loosened his tie and then carefully unfastened the top button of his perfectly pressed shirt. She could do this seduction thing, couldn't she? Surely she could find a way to rattle Jackson's oh-so-admirable control.

Allowing her voice to hit a breathy note, she gazed up at him. "You let me teach you how to go a little wild.''

Maybe part of her hoped he'd back down. That way she'd never have to risk having a good time with a man all wrong for her. Of course, that was the same part of her that also wished they could have just slept together tonight after that amazing kiss. They could have taken the edge off all those lusty feelings zinging back and forth between them without the messy complications bound to follow in a relationship.

To his credit, Jackson never even hesitated. "You've got yourself a deal, Summer. And lucky for us I just happen to know the most legally binding way to seal the bargain in the absence of a notary." His hands materialized on her shoulders, the hardened palms providing a pleasing rasp against her skin.

"You do?" She was too busy worrying about whether she'd just made a crazy decision based on physical attraction to follow Jackson's thinking.

But as his gaze narrowed to her mouth and he loomed closer, Summer realized what he had in mind.

And maybe it wasn't too late to tumble all gorgeous six-foot-plus of Jackson Taggart into bed tonight.

HER KISS seared his insides. Hell, his outsides were pretty much on fire, too.

Must. Not. Hit. The. Sheets.

Jackson clung to the thought as Summer tugged at his shoulders and wriggled her way toward the lush red satin bed.

He never should have indulged in another kiss. He'd only wanted a little taste of her to tide him over until tomorrow and make her anticipate their day together.

But she'd thrown herself into the lip lock with no restraint, and now she proved to be every inch the bedroom goddess he had pegged her for when he first spotted her in the lounge tonight.

If he allowed her to woo him into her bed, his gut told him she'd skate out of their date tomorrow and he'd never have the chance to learn anymore about her.

Damn it, he wanted more from her than that.

He wanted to see what she had in mind for teaching him how to go wild. No doubt, he'd have a few surprises in store for her in that department, but he was perfectly content letting her take the lead if it made her feel more comfortable.

And just maybe part of him looked forward to thumbing his nose at his family, the press and all his government contacts pressuring him to run in a race he hadn't had time to really even consider.

Dating unconventional Summer would certainly be a public declaration that he was tired of being the golden-boy bachelor.

After too many years of dating ambitious society debs who played all the same games as him, he'd have a hell of a time smashing that picture-perfect image of himself.

If he wanted any of those things to materialize, however, he needed to stay out of Summer's bed tonight.

Pulling away from her sultry embrace despite the flames licking over him, Jackson searched for a breath that wasn't laden with the musky floral scent of her.

Found none.

Much to his male satisfaction, her eyes remained closed for a long moment afterward. It would be so easy to resume their kiss, to follow the irresistible pull of her…

Desperate for a way to keep things under control before he lost it completely, Jackson's gaze seized on the pile of lingerie on the other side of the room.

Thank you, God.

"So is it my turn to ask the questions yet?" He

traced a line down the bare skin of her arm and slipped his hand around her fingers. Her nails were short, painted with barely-there polish. She wore a silver band woven with a Celtic pattern on one thumb.

She blinked twice, tucked a strand of silky blond hair behind one ear. "Ask away."

"Is that your lingerie over there?" His loosened tie and unbuttoned collar didn't make him feel any less hot. And although Summer's lingerie collection wasn't exactly safe conversational territory, it was a damn sight better than falling into bed with her before he could find out more about her.

"I chose the pieces, but they're all going to be specialty amenities and props for the bordello." She eased her fingers from his grip and made her way toward the coffee table where the mountain of silk, satin and velvet presided. "Some are vintage and some are new, but they're all reminiscent of nineteenth-century bordello garb."

To illustrate, she held up a creamy-colored corset thing edged in black lace. Black satin garters dangled from the bottom.

"Very nice." He peered from the creamy corset to the crimson lace-up garment Summer was wearing. "It's sort of like what you have…on."

An image of those garters hugging her thighs blasted into his brain in full-blown color. His throat promptly dried to dust.

A wicked smile kicked up the corners of her mouth. "It's exactly what I have on. Same vendor, different color. I have to admit this job is dangerous to my personal budget, but I find a lot of gorgeous clothes and furnishings this way. Did you know I'm the ambiance coordinator for the club?''

He hadn't known, and he scrambled to pick up the conversational thread before he drowned in sensual visions of Summer's pale thighs draped in black satin and lace.

"Is that like a decorator?" His voice sounded strangled even in his own ears.

"The decorating is just a part of my job. I have a hand in the total sensual experience of Club Paradise from the food and the music to the colors, party themes, flowers..." She laid the creamy corset back on the pile of silky undergarments. "...and occasionally, lingerie."

The comment called to mind snippets of the conversation he'd heard between Summer and her girlfriend earlier. He happened to know the bordello was her favorite fantasy room.

"So did you come up with the concepts for the hotel suites?" Crossing the thick pile carpet to where she stood near the sitting area, Jackson peered around the room with new eyes, taking in the details of the lush seating, the silver-plated cigar box on the night stand, the framed sepia-toned photographs depicting half-clad women from another era.

"I brainstormed with my partners to come up with the themes and then I ran with them." She reached into the open cherry armoire and pulled out a padded hanger. With careful fingers, she draped a frothy pink scrap of lace across the padding and hung the costume in the closet. "I'm proud to claim full responsibility for the bordello however."

He recalled her wistful remark to her friend about

being totally overwhelmed and at a man's whim. Dangerous, forbidden knowledge he had no right to have heard.

Still, he'd trade his stellar track record as a trial lawyer for a chance to be a part of Summer's fantasies.

"You should be." He walked over to the silver cigar box to prevent his restless body from getting closer to her again. He didn't know how much longer he could be in the same room with Summer without touching her again. Removing one of the Cuban smokes from its velvet-lined case he sniffed the aroma. "I'm no expert on the historical authenticity, but if you were aiming for a design that promotes intense sexual thoughts, the ambiance of the bordello is dead-on."

Summer watched Jackson finger the cigar before replacing it in the box, his words causing her blood to pump a bit faster through her veins. She paused as she reached for a wine-colored merry widow and straightened.

Did he think to play games with her that he would rev her engines so acutely and then turn away?

"Actually, I'm beginning to wonder if I failed miserably in the design now that I've shared this room with a man for the first time. How come a room that promotes intense sexual thoughts doesn't inspire any actual…sex?"

Jackson flipped the lid closed on the cigar box. When his gaze met hers across the room, his eyes glittered with new heat. "Never let it be said I left this room uninspired tonight."

As he turned more fully toward her, the tent-effect of his trousers told her just how inspired he'd grown.

Realizing she was staring, she struggled to lift her gaze. Failed.

Had *she* had that affect on him?

Suddenly she felt quite inspired herself. She blurted the first thought that entered her mind. ''So why leave the room at all?''

The question hung there, an echoing reminder of her recklessness.

When he didn't answer right away, Summer couldn't resist the urge to keep right on talking, thinking out loud. ''Or is that too impulsive for you, Jackson? As a public figure, do you need to script out your every move ahead of time, or can you ever act according to whim and…inspiration?''

''I can act on impulse when the situation calls for it.'' He crossed the room, his slow, deliberate steps a physical reminder of the way he carefully crafted his next move. ''But when something is very important to me, I'd prefer to rely on well-thought out strategy.''

The implication that she—a free-spirited gypsy who'd never stayed anywhere longer than six months until now—might rank as important to him caught her off guard. She'd had to say goodbye to too many friends in her life to risk her emotions with someone who thought she might be important. Much easier to keep things simple. And okay, maybe a little superficial.

''How am I ever going to teach you to go wild with that kind of attitude?'' Planting a fist on her hip she licked her lips, flirting openly. She still held out hope she could sway him to break his rigid ideas of how this relationship was going to progress. ''You must realize careful strategy is directly opposed to everything that being wild represents.''

"I think we can effectively co-exist on both ends of the spectrum." He halted a few steps from her, almost as if he drew a mental line between them.

What would he do with all his damn strategy if she plastered herself against him right now and let her body to the talking?

Then again, according to the local newspaper, Jackson Taggart had made a name for himself in Miami with thorough trial preparation and an ambitious career strategy. He'd left the lucrative family law practice at a young age to work in the D.A.'s office, quickly accumulating an amazing track record as a prosecutor.

Summer admired that kind of drive even if she'd never possessed it herself. Old self-doubts threatened as she wondered if she'd be able to claim half as much success in her own new business. Could she—the woman who'd held twelve different jobs before this one—ever stick with something long enough to make it a success?

Tamping down the twinge of insecurity, she crossed his physical line to stand toe-to-toe with him. "Are you prepared to settle for just co-existing when we could be doing so many other more interesting things?"

To prove her point, she laid her hand against his chest and walked southward with her fingers.

Jackson caught her wrist as she hit his belt, his fierce grip an indication that she might have pushed him to his personal limit.

They stared at one another in the swirl of blues music and the sea of red velvet, silent for a tense moment.

Finally, Jackson released her wrist to a more gentle hold, soothing her skin and her racing pulse with the pad of his thumb.

"How about tonight you go along with my strategy and tomorrow I'll adapt to your impulses?" His voice was even but his breath huffed out in a ragged sigh.

Nodding, she agreed, even as she wondered if she'd lost her mind.

Clearly this steely-willed Taurus man was all wrong for her artistic, move-with-the-flow Aquarian self. Even the stars said she had no business dating Jackson on a boat or anywhere else.

As much as Summer looked forward to the freedom of the waves and the lure of the water tomorrow, she also couldn't help but fear she was already in way over her head.

# 4

_____

*Sensual inspiration may ambush you when you least expect it.*

"I MISS the hot-tub meetings," Summer groused to her co-owners the next afternoon in one of their frequent executive sessions. Today they were taking care of business in the vacant and half-finished Sensualist's Suite. At least, she'd be taking care of business for another couple of hours before she saw Jackson again. "How come we've created one of the most hedonistic playgrounds on South Beach and now we're relegated to the rooms that still have scaffolding and paint brushes?"

Lainie Reynolds, an attorney with shrewd business sense and a thirst to take revenge on her cheating ex-husband by turning his former club into a raging success, tossed Summer a spiral notebook with a pen wedged in the wire coil. "Because now we're open for business. We can't indulge ourselves in the hot tubs anymore. Personally, I'm not in any hurry to put my thirty-year-old bod on display beside the swarm of European models and twenty-one-year-old party monsters in tangas by the downstairs pool."

Summer cracked open the spiral notebook with a huff. "Please. You could give them all lessons with your silk cover-up and your high heels.'' She spared a glance for her sleek blond partner as Lainie passed out notebooks to their co-owners as the other women entered the suite. Lainie's black robe had a fire-breathing dragon embroidered on the back, her toes painted the same fire-engine red shade as the mythical creature stitched across her shoulders. ''You've got some sort of Grace Kelly meets Grace Jones thing going on there. I think you could hold your own with the beach babes by the pool.''

''Still mad we can't sit in the hot tubs anymore?'' Brianne Wolcott strode into the partially renovated suite, her auburn hair a sharp contrast to her cool gray skirt and neatly tucked white blouse. She slid off one high heel to plunge her toe in the man-made brook that streamed through the exotic room. ''Why don't you just dip your feet in the stream for your water fix?''

Summer didn't mention that her water fix was going to come from another source today. She'd never been the type to keep secrets about the men she dated before, but something about this date with Jackson struck her as more tenuous than her one-night interludes with surfer studs in the past. ''Putting my feet in the water isn't the same. I just don't want our group to turn into some rigid corporate crowd where we feel like we need to sit around a conference table wearing power suits.''

Giselle Cesare, the fiery Italian head chef and fourth owner of Club Paradise, patted Summer's shoulder as she waved a pink pastry box under her nose. ''But at least if we ever do sit around a conference table, I can personally guarantee you we'll still be munching on erotic confections to keep things lively.''

Summer's spirits lifted slightly. She wasn't joking about her fear of going corporate. She'd never be able to make it in a job where she couldn't occasionally don overalls and do a little spackling and tiling on her own walls, damn it.

''Really?'' She reached for the pastry box as both Lainie and Brianne hovered closer. ''And just what naughty treat do you have for us today?''

Giselle's only response was a sly smile, urging Summer's fingers to flick open the box and see for herself.

And there, nestled on a bed of wax paper and covered in delicate frosting, were the chef's prize delectable... ''Kama Sutra cookies.'' Brianne and Summer breathed the words with similar hushed reverence.

Even Lainie let out a momentary sigh of longing before she asked, ''Shouldn't we save these for guests?''

''No. These are actually a few of the flawed ones. You'll note the extra arm on one of them, the anatomically impossible position on another, and one cookie depicts a very huge male member thanks to a slip of my wrist while painting.'' She rolled her eyes as she began handing out the cookies. ''I finally found time to make a batch despite my brothers being underfoot all week trying to convince me the club is no place for an innocent young lady like me. Can you imagine? So I finally decided to put them to work as long as they were here. I made Renzo clean the kitchen and Nico organize the pantry, which gave me tons of time to paint my cookies.''

Summer gazed down at the sweet in her hand, which depicted a woman kneeling before a man as she pleasured him. Sure enough, there was an extra arm in there, but the work remained lovely. The woman's long dark hair fell over her shoulder to graze the man's thigh while the man's head fell back in sensual abandon. "Damn, but you are a genius, Giselle. If you ever decide to try painting on canvas instead of sugar cookies, I'll be the first in line to buy up all your artwork."

And how. The simple picture was enough to give a woman sweet shivers. Especially if she already had a virile, gorgeous man on her mind.

Lucky for her, Jackson had said he was ready to go a little wild with her, and she had managed to shuffle her day off so she could take full advantage of their time on the boat today. Would he be amenable to letting her try out the sensual position depicted on her cookie, she wondered?

Perhaps the sexy thoughts were catching because Lainie was fanning herself as she stared down at her treat. "I think I'm going to frame mine just in case I forget how it's done. I mean, don't get me wrong, I'm thrilled to be divorced…" Her eye lingered on Giselle for a moment, making them all tense since Giselle had unwittingly had an affair with Lainie's husband in an earlier lifetime. "…but the lack of sex is less appealing."

Clearing her throat, Summer removed the cap from her pen before a catfight broke out in the Sensualist's Suite. She needed to get her mind off Jackson anyway and focus on the business she'd worked so hard to bring to life. "Maybe we should get down to the work at hand then?"

She really shouldn't be letting Jackson Taggart dominate her thoughts. She'd undertaken the mission of Club Paradise to prove to herself that she could be successful and have fun doing it. No way would she let a man overshadow that dream already.

But nearly an hour later, Summer feared for her dream.

According to the dismal income figures Lainie had shared with them all, business wasn't booming as much as they needed yet. Sure, the nightclub was hopping and the lines to enter the Moulin Rouge Lounge were impressive, but the hotel suites weren't yet booked to capacity and the women were running on a thin margin for loss given how much they'd each strapped themselves to personally invest in Club Paradise.

To keep them financially solvent, they needed to fill every room every night and reserve them well into the next six months.

Of course, Lainie had a plan for a massive promotion campaign that included assignments for everyone. Hence the spiral notebooks.

"Brianne, you can call some of your contacts from the film industry and see if anyone wants to use the resort as a setting for a movie." Lainie never asked questions. She issued orders.

"It can be difficult to—" Brianne started, but Lainie was already on to the next assignment.

"Giselle can muscle some of the food magazines about reviewing the restaurants at the club. We need a food critic in here—or several—so we can get some write-ups. And Summer has already contacted a travel magazine, so I'm sure we can expect a visit from them any day.'' Lainie tapped her silver pen against her yellow legal pad as she perched on a corner of the scaffolding crowding the half-finished room. "We really need the positive press. We've been in the papers ever since the first Rat Pack embezzler was put behind bars. Mel Baxter's trial has been calling into question the club's reputation and making out-of-towners more leery of staying here. If we want to keep our heads above water this first year, we have to start fighting back.''

Lainie couldn't have issued a more powerful call to action as far as Summer was concerned. She wouldn't—couldn't—fail in her first attempt to pour something of herself into her work. Always before she'd taken jobs to bide the time, jobs to make money, jobs to allow her to travel around and see the country.

Her work with Club Paradise was about more than that. She didn't want to be a gypsy forever. She wanted to prove to herself that she could stay put long enough to accomplish something important, something special, something that contained a piece of her long after she'd gone.

So even though her nerves throbbed with expectation at the thought of seeing Jackson again, she needed to delay her trip to his boat until she placed another call to *Wanderlust* magazine. For that matter, she would need to delay the date if she couldn't get business sewn up first.

Because no matter how much she wanted to get a little wild with South Beach's hottest politician, her job had to come first.

"DON'T YOU THINK your career needs to come first, Jack?"

The voice of his future campaign manager rasped through Jackson's cell phone, making a point he damn well didn't want to hear. Fortunately, Jackson had walked through life masking annoyance for the sake of his family's political ambitions many times and he smoothly lowered the small wooden gangplank on his sailboat while he set Lucky Adams straight.

"I'm still determining my next career move, so it's actually *always* in the forefront of my mind." Though that might be stretching the truth a bit, since he was keeping one eye on the pier for Summer's long blond hair and tiny pink braids the whole time he prepped his boat to hit the water. "I'm not going to make a lot of campaign plans until I'm one-hundred-percent sure this is what I want."

"Every day you wait, your chances of winning decrease." Smooth-talking Lucky was a slick manager in his early thirties who'd already developed a reputation for building his clients into heavy hitters. He proceeded to launch into a well-articulated diatribe about the dire state of Jackson's political future while Jackson checked the fuel tank and rolled up the canvas tarp covering the seats in the back of the boat.

He didn't need to hear the tirade again to know he was taking chances with his future by putting off his announcement to run in the state legislature race. But he'd been in a tailspin ever since the scandal involving his father had been uncovered. Ever since he'd learned his father's entire political career—from his stint as an FBI assistant director to his term as a high-powered judge—was based on lies and deception.

Sort of robbed the job of some of its sheen.

Add to that the fact that the media would dissect all his father's mistakes in relation to Jackson's campaign and the whole proposition became less enticing.

And then, there was Summer...

Jackson spied her just as she jumped into his mind. She strode down the pier and onto the long wooden dock, her high heels traded for a pair of bright white tennis shoes with no socks and endlessly long legs tucked into denim shorts. A tiny white T-shirt with a bright blue emblem for water—the astrological thing again—didn't quite reach the hem of the shorts. In one hand she held a shiny chrome cell phone that she now tucked inside her purse.

The pink braids from last night had vanished without a trace. Today her hair was all blond and gathered in a loose ponytail which she had tossed over one shoulder.

She would have looked almost conventional if not for the silver sunglasses she sported. The frames around her eyes were shaped like seashells and coated with glitter.

His brain lost all focus as he absorbed the sight of her—sexy and eccentric, a definite original. Relief charged through him with as much force as anticipation, because up until that moment he hadn't been entirely sure she would show.

Yet here she was.

"You there, Jackson?" The smooth-talking masculine voice on the other end of his phone jarred him.

"I need to head out now, Lucky." The words fell off his lips with wooden heaviness, his brain on a totally different path that had nothing to do with forming words. "I'll stop by there later tonight and we'll figure out when to schedule the press conference."

He disconnected the call and turned off the ringer for good measure. Jogging two steps down into the berth he tossed the phone on the bed in his stateroom. Out of sight, out of mind. He'd told Summer he would be impulsive today, hadn't he? Taking time off from politics—both family and professional—would be a first for him.

And he would gladly be much *more* spontaneous with the incentive of Summer's seductive invitations. Not that he'd be leaving his strategy-making ways behind him. He had goals to accomplish today above and beyond his foray into being impetuous.

Like making sure Summer didn't bolt after their one and only date.

"Over here!" He waved to her as she looked around the marina. The tails of his unbuttoned shirt caught the breeze. He docked his boat on the intercoastal waterway between Miami Beach and the city of Miami. He lived in a high-rise condo on Collins Avenue for that very reason—the apartment came with a docking option.

She waved in return, her smile lighting up her whole face and making his breath hitch in his chest.

Her walk commanded his complete attention as she strode down the dock toward his boat. She had the bouncing, full-of-life stride of a runway model, only none of Summer's energy was manufactured for show. She radiated life and energy like a neon sign—bright and flashy.

"Did you find the place all right?" he called as she neared the gangplank. He'd really wanted to pick her up today. It was a date after all, damn it. But she'd been adamant about meeting him there.

Determined to keep him at arm's length.

Jackson was equally determined she wouldn't want to after today. To that end, he moved to greet her as soon as she stepped onto the boat, knowing it would be a minor miracle if he could keep his hands to himself for more than five seconds.

But if he ever wanted to make Summer's sexy fantasy come true, to fulfill her secret longing to be sensually overpowered, he needed to get closer to her first. Gain her trust. Create a relationship.

Hell, he'd have to invest plenty of time and a scary amount of emotion to make that happen for her, but ever since he'd heard her confide that private wish to her girlfriend, Jackson had been consumed by the need to experience that moment with her.

"Are you kidding? It was a piece of cake." She steadied herself on the dock's wooden railing as she stepped onto the plank. "And your valet parked my car for free in exchange for a one-night VIP pass to Club Paradise. Definitely a good trade."

He took her hand as she balanced herself, drawing her onto the boat—and satisfyingly closer to *him.*

"A very good trade," he agreed as she set foot on board mere inches from him. She was shorter today, which made sense given her lack of heels. But she packed as much firepower as ever with one killer smile and her perfect lips.

He contemplated her mouth at the same time he debated a kiss even though it wasn't time for that yet. She was near enough where he could almost...

Before he could act, she stepped back, releasing his

hand and giving him a sharp wake-up call to get his head on straight.

Damn.

Impulsiveness was *not* his strong suit. Stick to strategizing. And damn it, he'd probably have to plan his moment of freaking spontaneity so he didn't get off track and start kissing her when he had no business kissing her.

Yet.

WHAT IN THE HELL was he thinking? Summer stared into Jackson's deep-blue eyes that put the murky color of the intercoastal water to shame and wondered just what was going on in the man's head.

Had she dreamed that moment of intense scrutiny, or had he really been contemplating a kiss just now?

And if so, Summer hadn't just been idiot enough to step away, had she?

Could she be anymore clueless? Or maybe she was just too accustomed to being in charge when it came to kissing and the physical pacing of a relationship.

"The boat is gorgeous," Summer blurted to cover the awkward moment, acting on impulse when she had no clue what she was doing. "Will you need help sailing it? Because I'm a total novice when it comes to boats."

"You think charming my valet is easy, wait till you try sailing." Jackson switched gears smoothly, letting her off the hook even though his eyes still contained a trace of something dark and edgy and hungry.

Why the hell hadn't she kissed him?

As he moved to start the boat's engine, Summer noted he looked more approachable today. Closer to the type of man she could see herself with even if he didn't have a single tattoo in sight. His suit and tie had been replaced by a pair of navy swim trunks. Maybe they could be categorized as conservative, but Summer rather approved of them since there was nothing about them that would in any way detract from his gorgeous bod full of tanned, toned muscles.

Any surfer would envy the abs she spied underneath his open cotton shirt. Summer's fingers itched to trace the etched network of sharply defined muscle. The sparse hair on his forearms and his legs was sun-bleached, a dead giveaway that the man spent plenty of time on the boat.

"In other words, you *are* putting me to work today?" She wrenched her gaze from Jackson's rather spectacular physique to eye the sails and rigging with trepidation as he untied the boat. "You know, even though I love the water and I've got the Aquarian thing going on, I'm not at all sure I can keep us both from drowning out there. You might be better off finding a more skilled partner."

Jackson didn't bother to hide the predatory gleam in his blue eyes as he steered them into the waterway. "I have the feeling you're *exactly* the partner I'm looking for."

He tossed her something across the deck which she caught automatically. A fat white tube—mega-sunscreen.

She stared at him, knowing she probably appeared as dazed and confused as she felt. Without a doubt, this day with Jackson was going to be very different from the few and far between one-night sex romps that had been the sum total of her dating life so far.

Still, Jackson didn't seem like a man teeming with strategies today. He simply looked like a guy ready to have fun.

And that she could relate to.

"Lather up, partner, I'm going to put you to work in a minute." He winked at her as they rounded a bend to cross under Collins Avenue and move the boat out into the Atlantic. "And while we're waiting to get into the water you can think about where you want to go today. I've got no preconceived plans and I'm ready to be Mr. Spontaneous. Just name your destination."

THREE HOURS LATER, Summer sprawled out on the nose of Jackson's boat, soaking up the natural heat therapy of the sun slowly sinking on the horizon. Her every muscle ached with use from her first sailing outing, but despite the minor pains she'd loved every second of being on the water.

Even now she thrilled to the feel of steady waves rocking the boat, her body rising and falling in time with the swaying craft where they had anchored.

Shading her eyes, she peered around for her sexy captain, a man who'd been entirely friendly and not in the least forward all afternoon. He'd disappeared below deck after throwing out the anchor just past six o'clock. Normally she'd be headed into work at the club about now, but with the night off, her time was her own.

"Where are we anyway?" she called, missing the proximity of his tanned muscles and—she had to admit—his company. Being with Jackson had been more than just physically titillating—although she never managed to lose sight of her attraction to him for even five seconds. The last few hours had also been fun.

He hadn't grown frustrated with her on the couple of instances where she hadn't grasped what he'd been explaining to her right away. Having been introduced to more new situations and rituals than she could count in her parents' merry-go-round of cult memberships, Summer knew that kind of patience and good humor were rare qualities.

And he *had* listened to her regarding their destination, proving himself spontaneous for today at least.

"We're right where you said you wanted to be," he called back in the moment before his head cleared the deck and she caught sight of him once again. "In the middle of nowhere."

He held out his arms to the seascape, as if to invite her inspection. Only then did she notice the bottle of champagne in one hand, the blue plastic cups in the other. His champagne hand pointed toward the tiny island where they'd seen one other boat anchored on the opposite side. His hand holding the cups stretched in the direction of the descending sun and the expanse of blue water.

"But where in the middle of nowhere? You must have a map that labels this sort of thing." Summer liked adventure, but she rather hoped they didn't venture into Bermuda Triangle territory or anything.

"I've got latitude and longitude coordinates." He hopped over the cockpit to join her on the bow, his bare feet stepping lightly on the white fiberglass. "And the boat's navigational equipment can tell us how to get back from wherever 'here' might be, but other than that, I don't have a clue where we are. The maps don't label every outcropping of land.''

She rolled to one side of the big beach towel she'd discovered beneath one of the bench seats, making room for him. ''I can't believe you don't know where we are and you're not freaking out about it.''

He pulled a face while he popped the cork on the champagne and sat down beside her. ''I don't make it a habit to freak out. Besides, I may not know where we are, but I know exactly how to get to my destination.''

The heated look he sent sizzling across the deck made her reel, instilled that out-of-control feeling that had her taking a mental step backward.

Scooping up the blue cups as she rose to her knees, Summer held them out for him to fill. ''Really? I had you pegged for the kind of guy who would lose it if somebody put your brown socks on the stack of your black socks.''

''Well you also thought I couldn't be impulsive, and just look at us sitting out in the middle of the Atlantic like refugees from *Gilligan's Island.* Having poured their drinks, he set the bottle aside and took one of the cups.

''You're right.'' She read the label on the champagne and sniffed. ''The Howells probably had a few bottles of Moët tucked in their suitcases, didn't they? I guess you're more of a wild man than I realized.''

Clinking his cup to hers, Jackson raised his drink in a toast. ''Here's to spontaneity.''

''Amen to that.'' Pleasure curled through her that had more to do with the sentiment and the moment than with having Jackson's supremely male body stretched out beside her.

Happiness.

Affection.

Her emotions gently churned along with the Atlantic, a constant back-and-forth motion that confused her. She wanted him. She feared getting involved with him on anything more than a physical level.

Jackson seemed to want her. But he didn't seem to want to get involved unless more than their bodies were engaged.

Yet he had to know they were all wrong for each other as he sat there—South Beach's golden boy—in his conservative blue trunks sipping top-shelf champagne. She lounged next to him in glitter sunglasses and a T-shirt she'd decorated with a home spin-art kit.

This relationship had doom written all over it if she were foolish enough to give him more than her body.

At least now that the boat had been anchored, the time seemed to have arrived where she could finally focus on just the physical.

Assuming of course, she could block out all those great memories of trimming sails, steering the rudder and playing on the ocean with Jackson as her guide.

Even as she reached for him, she knew she didn't stand a chance.

## 5

*A word of caution about unleashing the beast...*

SUMMER'S HAND landed on his chest, the gentle weight carrying as much impact to his self-control as an overturned verdict.

As for strategy...

Jackson couldn't remember if he'd even had one for today. He gulped his drink a hell of a lot faster than he should have, scrambling to remember any rational plan he might have concocted with regard to Summer.

Right now, as they lounged together like a couple of castaways without another soul in sight, Jackson felt a downright primitive urge to claim her.

"You seem to have made great strides in the impulsive department today, Taggart." Propped on one elbow, Summer stretched out on her side, her drink safely stowed in one of the rings that served as cup holders peppered around the bow. Her fingertips grazed his abs, their feather weight causing his skin to tighten, his muscles to tense.

"Maybe I've always been the impetuous type and you just couldn't see beyond the suit and tie last night." He downed the rest of his champagne and slid his glass into the holder alongside hers.

"The perfectly pressed suit and tie," she amended,

her hand remaining still but sensually lethal. "Let's not forget that. Somehow, I don't think my vision was faulty last night. I'm guessing today's spontaneity is a stretch for you."

"Do you pigeonhole everyone you meet, Summer Farnsworth?" He watched as her long ponytail slid over her shoulder to cradle her neck like a scarf. The ends brushed the red terry cloth beach blanket she'd unearthed from somewhere and laid over the bow.

She shrugged, disturbing the resting place of the blond mane for only a moment. "I've moved around a lot in my life and I've found it helpful to draw some basic comparisons when you're in a strange place or introduced to new people. I evaluate what I don't know by the standards of what I do know. And quite frankly, any time I've ever met a guy with a shirt so crisp you could use it for stationary at midnight, that generally means the man underneath is a perfectionist, a man who embraces order and, I'll admit, maybe a little rigid."

Jackson wasn't touching the rigid comment. No way. No how. Not when Summer's long tanned limbs lay a foot away from his, and his body was moments away from giving new meaning to the word.

The air between them crackled with unspoken messages and a sea of want. And although he was a hell of a lot more interested in the conversation of body language going on right now, he also felt the need to respond to her comment, since Summer obviously didn't understand him at all.

He could ignore the body talk for five more minutes to correct Summer's mistaken impressions, couldn't he? Taking deep breaths, he focused on moving some oxygen to his brain so he stood a chance of thinking straight.

"Well, it looks as if this time your system deceived you, Summer. I request an obscene amount of starch in my shirts because ninety percent of the photos of me that land in the paper are taken when I go out at night. Having a wrinkled shirt in the *Herald* is something akin to Dante's sixth circle according to Taggart family lore. It may be family wisdom I guess I never bothered to question, but it sure as hell isn't an indication of being uptight."

"Oh no?" Summer's fingers swirled over his chest in an idle circle that set a match to his bloodstream.

The body-language conversation grew increasingly difficult to ignore.

Had they talked for the requisite five minutes yet?

"Definitely not." He pivoted onto his side, hoisting himself up on one elbow to be eye-to-eye with her. When he noticed her seashell sunglasses still resting on her nose, he lifted them by the bridge piece and resettled them in her hair so he could see her whole face. Read her expression.

Her gray eyes communicated a restless heat, a definite hunger, in an eloquent language all their own.

To hell with five minutes.

"Let me put it this way," he whispered, angling his body closer to hers. "Would an uptight guy try to kiss you out of your clothes right here in the open on the bow of a boat?"

Her eyes widened to a satisfying degree before they softened, narrowed. "Maybe not," she sank back against the fiberglass hull, an invitation if ever he saw one. "But I'll bet an arrogant guy might try it."

"Guilty." He followed her down to kiss her, to taste those perfect lips on his own terms and in his own time now that there was no rush. No real underlying agenda other than to convince her to see him again.

And again.

The moment his mouth grazed hers he was right back to the searing point, almost as if he'd returned to that moment last night when they'd been teetering inches from the bordello bed, both so hot and ready they nearly combusted.

He covered Summer's lush little frame with his own, his shoulders blocking the setting sun from her eyes, her face. Anchoring himself above her on his elbows, he carefully angled her chin to provide himself with the best taste of her.

So sweet.

Like spun sugar melting on his tongue, the flavor of Summer infused his senses. He could have allowed his eyes to slide closed to concentrate on that delectable experience, but he needed to see her, too.

Her eyes had fluttered once and then sealed themselves shut. Of course, she was the kind of woman who would give herself with abandon. In fact, he'd counted on it.

Now her body arched against him, her breasts rising to meet the surface of his chest even though he'd tried to hold himself back just a little longer. One day he vowed he would go slowly with her, absorb every nuance of her body and every facet of her sensual response like a damn scholar. But today wasn't the time for that.

Not when her soft arms were slipping around his neck and her thighs slid a restless dance against his.

They sure as hell were saying a lot to one another now. This was the language they were both most fluent in, this electric glide of bodies and soft mating of mouths. Although to the casual observer they looked diametrically opposed, with Summer's glitter glasses or her pink clip-on braids next to his conservative suits, they were crooning in perfect harmony right here as he kissed his way down the delicate curve of her throat.

When he reached the hollow at the base of her neck, he lingered, steadying her hip with one hand as he lapped at the salty skin. The water rocked the boat beneath them, a constant motion that lulled him at the same time it caused his hips to suddenly brush hers.

Their gasps mingled, a mutual throaty plea for more.

Summer's eyes flew open at the contact, her gray eyes dark with longing and focused solely on him. "If this is the way you talk a woman out of her clothes, Taggart, you're doing a damn good job."

As if to illustrate her point she tugged her shirt over her head, leaving her clad in the simple white bikini top for all of two seconds before she untied the skimpy strings and released amazingly generous breasts for such a lithe body.

Rapidly losing any ability to slow down or savor, Jackson cupped the soft mounds in his hands as he took her in his mouth, drew on her harder than he'd intended.

Summer only moaned louder, wriggled more and reached for the snap on her denim shorts.

The woman was a walking, talking wet dream and he had just entered fantasy territory. Especially when she delved into a pocket of those shorts of hers and withdrew a foil package that could only contain one thing.

Could a man ask for more than sexy—prepared— Summer Farnsworth peeling off her clothes on the deck of his boat?

Praying no fishing parties would be curious about this corner of the Atlantic today, Jackson watched hungrily as he caught his first glimpse of white satin bikini bottoms so tiny he had to wonder if she went Brazilian underneath them.

But no, his avid gaze took in the wispy blond hair cut in the shape of a heart as she tugged the other half of her bathing suit down her thighs, too. And then he almost wished he hadn't looked because he feared he had about ten seconds to get inside her before he lost all control.

Damn. Damn. Damn.

"How does a girl go about getting you naked, Taggart?" Summer looked up at him through coyly lowered lashes, her tongue circling her lips in blatant invitation as she reached for *his* shorts.

Holy hell.

He had an image of his bare ass on the national news tomorrow morning. Or even worse, Summer exposed to the world because he hadn't been more careful, more considerate.

Unable to discuss his plan or ask for input, Jackson scooped her bare body up off the deck and into his arms before his brain became completely paralyzed with sex. He made damn sure she still clutched that foil package in her hand however. He wasn't *that* far gone.

Thankful he'd grown up on the water, he blessed his years spent on the family boat for his ability to make serious time across the hull now with a naked woman in his arms. He angled around a boom and landed them in back of the cockpit, sprawling them both over the deck cushions strewn on the floor.

With ten more steps he could have made it to the complete privacy of the cabin below, but they were sheltered from the eyes of passersby here and time was of the essence. Summer had ditched every shred of *her* clothes, yet she looked up at him as if she wanted to devour *him* whole.

Christ, she didn't know the meaning of *want*.

In some vague recesses of his brain he realized that, true to her mission, Summer had succeeded in her attempt to make him go wild today. He'd never gotten naked this fast with a woman in his life. He just might be a convert to this spontaneity thing after all.

"I can't wait," he muttered the words as he shucked his swim trunks, the sight of her slender form and lush curves switching his impulses into overdrive.

Summer forced herself to remain utterly still even when her hands itched to touch the newly bared terrain of Jackson Taggart's formidable bod. She didn't want to distract whatever train of thought charged through his mind right now because she relished every minute of in-control and out-of-control Jackson.

"I'd have to hurt you if you waited," she assured him, barely able to restrain herself. She'd never expected him to respond so quickly to her horizontal striptease, but the results were more than gratifying. Somehow by indulging her own wants, she'd received the added benefit of being able to get past that practical reserve of his to the wild man beneath.

She'd unleashed the beast, and, even better, he had a tattoo.

Before she could get a good look at the black-and-white circle on the inside of his hip, he lay down beside her, half on top of her, his weight a welcome pressure against the empty edginess between her thighs.

She hadn't been with a guy in forever, but she remembered enough of her encounters to know she didn't usually get wound up this high, this fast. She stole his hands from her hips to glide them up her ribs to cup her breasts as she reclined on the blue seat cushions strewn about the floor.

His touch felt so hot, his hands so textured against her smooth skin, as if her sensitive flesh could divine every loop and ripple of his fingerprints. Yet as soon as she moved his hands to one place, her body ached for that touch in another place. She couldn't possibly get enough of the feel of him.

He kissed her then, diverting her attention to the slick sweep of his tongue over hers. A shiver raked through her, her whole focus concentrated on that sweetly sexual act.

A moan escaped her lips, resonated in her chest. Jackson responded by transferring his hands to her thighs, gently spreading her.

Fire licked her most sensitive places as his tongue nudged her in time with his cock. When he angled his head to gain better access to her mouth, his hips thrust forward, finding more intimate access, as well.

It was too much.

Sensory overload.

Summer felt the heat gather in her belly and tighten into the hard knot of desire that threatened to unravel any moment. She broke the kiss, needing to slow herself down, to focus on just one thing at a time.

"Too potent," she managed, having no clue if the phrase would mean anything to him but she was too wrapped up in a flood of sensation to interpret anything *he* might be feeling at the moment.

He withdrew from her just a little and then edged his way back inside, stretching her and filling her completely.

"You're telling me?" he whispered the words against her ear as he grazed his chest over hers. Her nipples beaded at the friction. "If I so much as look down at you and see that heart shaved between your legs, I'm going to detonate."

She smiled into the warm skin of his neck, pleased she wasn't the only one on edge. "You liked the heart?"

"Jesus, I think I might have passed out at the sight."

Her giggle turned to a gasp when he levered himself higher, creating exquisite pressure against her. He reached between their bodies to touch her, his thick finger gliding easily against the slick wetness of her.

There was a good chance her eyes crossed just before they slid shut to concentrate on that magic wrought by his hands and his cock. The setting sun and the miles of ocean around them became a distant memory with the more pressing sensory input nudging her higher and higher until she unreeled, spinning out across the water in a hot flash of delicious release.

She didn't realize she had screamed until her throat went hoarse with the shout, but she slowly grew aware enough to realize when Jackson found his own rhythm moments later.

Slumping over her with muscles that steamed like a horse's after a good morning run, Jackson lay utterly still and silent.

Having zero experience with silence, she rushed to fill it up. "That was amazing."

"Unprecedented." He offered up the sentiment seemingly without moving a muscle.

"Totally profound." Summer's hands longed to venture over him, to experience every hard masculine plane at her leisure. Oddly, the gesture struck her as too personal, too intimate.

Something about her words seemed to catch his ear, capture his attention. He hoisted himself up on an elbow. "That's it exactly. Profound."

He stared down at her with those wildly intense eyes of his, creating more intimacy with a look than she ever could have mustered by rubbing his back.

Offering up a weak smile, she remembered why she'd always tried to avoid romantic entanglements. Her heart was damned susceptible. Other women caught colds, she caught romance. And to her way of thinking, romance and all of the idealized thinking that went along with it had a hell of a lot longer recovery time than the sniffles.

"Maybe I'd better go grab my clothes before they blow right off the deck." She edged out from underneath him, disrupting their haven of seat cushions and banging Jackson in the knee as she went.

"Wait." Jackson caught her wrist just before she got away.

Damn.

She had no clue how to cool things down to a comfortable level of camaraderie after the heated encounter they had just shared. Then again, she had even less of a clue how to conduct a wildly passionate long-term affair.

Maybe she would be interested in that one day, with a different sort of man, but not right now. Not with this man—

Ohmigod, major panic attack on the horizon.

"Are you okay?" Jackson was already on his feet, his magnetic blue eyes missing nothing as they roamed over her. "I know the sex was pretty damn transporting and all that, but you look sort of far away." His grip on her wrist loosened, his thumb stroking over the back of her hand in soothing circles. "Have a seat and I'll go grab your things."

He slid on his trunks for the trip across the boat. No surprise there, his natural penchant for good strategy probably made him a hell of a lot more prudent than her.

Nodding, she squeezed her eyes shut tight as his footsteps moved away from her. Where were her damn crystals when she needed them? She should be grounding and centering herself right now instead of flying around with her emotions in a state of Aquarian upheaval.

Jackson would surely think she was a mess. Which she was. She just hadn't fully comprehended how frightened she'd been of a relationship until just now.

Although the idea of commitment with a grown-up

who would care about her held definite appeal from afar, whenever she ventured close to such a thing she quickly recalled why it wasn't right for her. All the people she'd counted on while growing up had—in some way or another—used her affections for their own gain. Such was the world of the cults her parents often chose. Even her first lover had turned out to be on a mission to gain her compliance in the Modern Druid Society.

Not that she held it against the Druids. She'd met nice people wherever she went, too, it was simply that the cult mindset bred an obsessive group mentality. One which Summer was certain she'd never fall victim to, yet here she was flipping out after the best sex of her life.

As she stood in the back of the boat watching Jackson scoop her clothes off the deck in the twilight, Summer decided she'd deal with her personal phobias another day. Right now, she just needed to get the boat headed back to shore so she could run from the sweet allure of South Beach's most eligible bachelor.

MISSION Keep the Anchor in the Water was about to commence even though Jackson didn't have a frigging clue how to reach his objective.

Hell, he wasn't even sure what weapons he had in his arsenal. What would keep her there with him long enough for round two tonight when her eyes communicated a clear desire to flee?

Taking his time picking up her clothes and retrieving the champagne bottle, he racked his brain for answers, solutions, strategies....

Damn. He'd settle for a vague idea at this point.

If only he could find a way to get close to her long enough to let chemistry kick in, he'd be golden. Putting them within three feet of one another was like an invitation to spontaneously combust, but from the cagey look in her eyes just a few moments ago, he wasn't so sure he'd be given an opportunity to get that close again.

"Need help?" she prompted from the other side of the windshield.

He glanced up from where he knelt on the deck. She had flicked on the light in the cockpit as if to ward off any chance of intimacy. Night had fallen over the Atlantic and the tiny patch of land they'd anchored near, yet Summer didn't seem in any hurry to let the romance of the darkened sea sway her.

Then, just when he'd started to honestly weigh the merits of the "running out of gas" routine, Jackson heard the rumble of another engine in the water.

A boat approached....

And just like that, a much better plan fell into place. A way to get close to Summer again, a way either to soothe her fears or else to let spontaneous combustion take its natural course.

Regardless, he'd end up with the desired result. Summer in his arms, in his bed and agreeing to see him at least one more time.

The plan seemed so good, he had to pinch himself to be sure he wasn't dreaming.

# 6

*Remember your prey is formulating strategies of his own.*

SUMMER REALLY HOPED she was dreaming.

Could she honestly be hearing the sound of another boat engine out on the water? Automatically, her arms went around her naked torso in the inky darkness as her eyes moved toward Jackson.

Loaded down with their clothes, drinking cups and the champagne bottle from the deck, Jackson edged around the windshield above the cockpit and stepped to the back where she waited.

Nervous now for reasons that had nothing to do with relationship phobias, Summer moved to help him with the burden, but he dumped it all in a heap at their feet. Forgoing any small talk, he hustled her toward the stairs leading to the cabin, propelling them below deck just as another boat rounded the tiny island where they'd anchored.

Headlights flashed into their boat, the high beam landing on Summer's bare thigh for a split second before the strong arms behind her shoved her into the anonymity of the darkness below.

As the other engine growled closer, Summer tried to move deeper into the cabin, away from the bright lights still visible even from below deck. An inflatable raft they'd used for tubing earlier in the day blocked the narrow hallway. Her body rebounded lightly off the small rubber craft, bouncing her back against Jackson's chest.

His deliciously naked chest.

She knew she shouldn't be responding to those sexy pecs, or any other appealing parts of the man in front of her. But as her heart jumped in her chest with their near miss above board, Summer relished the adrenaline rush of their naughty encounter pounding through her. The thrill of almost being caught had plenty of appeal for her inner bad girl.

The salty smell of the ocean faded down in the tiny berth. The close quarters and body heat enhanced the coconut aroma of their sunscreen, the strawberry fragrance of her shampoo, the musky scent of his aftershave. Summer turned in his arms, close enough to him that she could see traces of five o'clock shadow at his jaw even in the darkness. She could almost feel the dull thud of his heart across the scant inch that separated them.

Her breath caught in her throat at being trapped against him. Her legs grew weak with want. And she didn't have to wonder if sex between them would be amazing anymore. She already knew just how perfect it would be, a fact that made her long for that seductive union all over again.

She might have been able to fight her own hunger. Probably not, but there was an outside chance that with all the panic she'd been feeling a few minutes ago she could have made a mad dash and escaped this close encounter unscathed.

But she didn't stand a chance of fighting it when Jackson looked at her with such all-consuming attention, his blue eyes turned dark and feral. Then his big, hot hands slipped around her waist, eased down to settle on the curve of her hip. Most of all, she couldn't argue with the way his body responded to their proximity—the immediate, tangible arousal....

How could she *not* melt all over him then and there?

Later, she would figure out how to dance her way out of this relationship gracefully. Later, after she'd had one more taste of Jackson's skillful kisses, one more encounter with those expert fingers of his.

She'd worked so hard and played so little the last few months—ever since investing her stake in Club Paradise. Surely she deserved this window of time simply to have fun.

Jackson's arms snaked around her in the dark, the long, lean lines of his body caging her against the soft fabric of the inflatable raft behind them.

Muted voices floated down to them from the passing boat above. From the change in the hum of the other craft's engine, it was obvious they had slowed down to look over Jackson's boat.

"Maybe it's someone local," Summer whispered just as his lips reached hers.

"We're far enough away from the island that no one can complain." He dipped to kiss the corner of her mouth, one hand reaching to cradle her chin, hold her steady.

Then her eyes fell shut and she couldn't think about the other boaters. A bright flash moved through her vision even with her eyes closed, but Summer didn't know if it was real or if the potent kisses were making her see stars already.

Somehow Jackson shoved enough of the raft aside to allow them access to a tiny stateroom lit only by the negligible moonlight drifting in one slim window. He elbowed them into the room and fell onto the bed against the two fat white pillows perched at the head, taking her with him. She landed on his chest, much to her delight. Although she'd had fantasies about being overpowered by a sexy male, she had never known any one well enough to play out that particular scenario. She felt more comfortable taking on the aggressor role herself.

Raising herself up on her hands to look down at Jackson reclined on the dark-gray coverlet, she shivered with her own power. Her stance above him was all the more exciting because she knew he could reverse their positions in a heartbeat if he wanted to.

Still, she had the feeling she could wield her own brand of strength here. By keeping this man totally entranced, she'd stay on top—literally and figuratively—for as long as she wanted.

"You look as though you're contemplating something wicked." Jackson curled those fabulous abs of his to nip at her breasts, licking a circle around one taut peak. "Should I be worried?"

"No." She shook her head, allowing the tips of her unbound hair to dance across his chest with the movement. "You should be very, very excited."

His breath hitched on a raspy note as she lowered her hand to explore the hard muscles of his belly. She smoothed her way beneath his swim trunks and over the tattoo on his hip she'd since discerned was the

Chinese symbol for yin and yang—the black-and-white blobs within a circle symbolizing balance. If she weren't half-afraid of deep and meaningful conversations while naked, she'd ask him about it. But somehow—ironically—that sounded too personal.

Instead she simply moved on in her fingertip quest, filing away the information for future reference. He hissed out a long sigh between his teeth as she edged her touch even further south.

Thanks to Giselle's Kama Sutra cookie, Summer had a very definite position in mind tonight, and she couldn't wait to try it out on Jackson.

Crawling backward on the built-in bed, she allowed her hair to tease a path down his torso and glide along his sides as she shoved his shorts off. The object of her mission lengthened, drawing closer to her lips as she hovered above him.

Wrapping tentative fingers around the base of him, she touched the tip with her tongue and circled him gently. Once. Twice. Then eased him into her mouth in a long, slow stroke.

His hands fisted lightly in her hair, as he hissed in a breath.

"Uncle." The strangled sound issued forth from his mouth in a dry plea. "Damn, woman. Uncle."

Tipping her head back, she ceased the intimate kiss and shook away the veil of her hair to look up at him. His gaze scorched her, his blue eyes so dark she could get lost in them. His hands slid down her shoulders and over her arms to haul her up on the bed beside him.

If ever she'd wanted to feel empowered, she'd just discovered the keys to the kingdom.

"But I don't have anymore condoms." She hadn't been exactly sure how to handle the lack until she recalled the Kama Sutra pose. Surely the method she'd embarked on had seemed like a natural way around that particular issue?

Jackson didn't answer her, opting instead to fall on top of her, pinning her to the mattress and the crisp gray bedspread with the weight of his body while his mouth found hers in the darkened stateroom.

His lips ravished hers, his tongue taking complete possession of her mouth, giving no quarter. Her head swam with the kiss, her body hungry for completion.

She might have forgotten all about the need for protection if he hadn't pressed a condom into her hand. Perhaps he'd reached into a nightstand while he'd been kissing her. Or maybe he'd produced it out of thin air. All she knew was that the man possessed magical hands and delightful talents when it came to sex.

When she rolled the condom on him, he didn't bury himself inside her straight away, however. She wanted to feel him deep within her, but he hovered above her, waiting, until she met his gaze in the dark stateroom.

Their eyes met in a moment of intimate connection while the boat rocked lightly beneath them. Only then, while he held her gaze with his, did he position himself between her thighs. Only then did he come inside her so slowly she thought she'd fly apart with wanting, the impossible stretching.

That moment of mental connection unsettled her even as the physical joining awakened her every sensual response. She closed her eyes, unwilling to contemplate anything more than the delicious heaviness sliding through her, the unbearable sweetness of his legs between hers, his fingers plying her sensitive skin….

The shout built in her throat until she had no choice but to scream with pleasure. Ripples of tingling satisfaction shook her, each one more delectable than the last, until finally they slowed, faded.

Once her body had quieted, she realized she still cried out, her hoarse voice still rasping out a quiet version of "yes, yes…" Good God, but she was out of her mind for the kind of resounding O's this man could produce in her.

What was there about their sensual bond that made her respond to him so deeply that the very core of her seemed to shudder with it?

The question was way too philosophical for the oh-so-physical plane she was enjoying now. Tossing aside the concern, she strained to open her eyes and found him watching her with a look of fascination.

"My God, you're gorgeous." Jackson smoothed his hand over Summer's cheek, absorbing the soft coolness and praying he could hold on to his restraint long enough to send her flying over that seductive ledge one more time tonight.

She smiled up at him with no hint of coyness, just one-hundred-percent, undiluted Summer-style honesty. "You're looking pretty damn good to me, too, right about now."

Her fingers flexed on his shoulders, her short nails gently digging into his skin.

He hadn't just meant she looked good. He'd meant she looked like a woman who belonged in his life for more than just a short-term fantasy that would bring them both pleasure.

But he didn't dare voice the thought. By now he'd gathered she was interested in sex but scared of anything that smacked of a relationship. Lucky for him, the intrusion of another boat near the water where they'd anchored had bought him enough time to think of a plan B for how to keep them together a little longer.

"Gorgeous?" She slid her hands over his chest, allowing her fingernails to rake his skin lightly. "If I'm so hot to trot in your eyes, Taggart, how come you're not going down for the count with me yet?"

She arched her back, raised her hips and squeezed her inner muscles just enough to make him all too aware he didn't have much time left.

Focus on the plan.

Mind on the goal.

He couldn't afford to rush this. Making Summer agree to see him again would require major stamina on his part.

"I think after conquering the sails today and patiently teaching me how to be impulsive, you ought to be compensated for your trouble." Gathering up her roaming hands, he lifted them above her head, secured them lightly against the headboard. "What do you say to pleasure in a two-to-one ratio tonight?"

"Two-to-one?" One delicate blond brow lifted at the suggestion. "As in, for every time you go into orbit, I go…twice?"

"Exactly." Sounded damn good in theory. Hell, what man wouldn't want to make it happen on a permanent basis?

But as Summer wrapped her legs around his, tugging him closer to her body despite her pinned arms, Jackson wondered if he needed to start making sacrifices to ancient sex gods in order to endure the pleasure.

"How can I possibly argue with that, counselor?" She rolled her hips beneath him in a move so good he nearly saw stars. A wicked smile spread over her face. "By all means, let the fun begin."

As he struggled to remember his own name, he knew he couldn't win this battle in bed. Not when he teetered so close to the edge himself. Not when Summer seemed to know *exactly* how close he already loomed.

"Not on your turf, babe." He withdrew from her and stood, then lifted her in his arms. "I need to even up the odds a little first."

She squealed as he hauled her into the bathroom adjoining the bedroom. They barely fit through the doorway with her strewn across his chest, but once they were inside, there was enough space to move around.

"Is this going to be kinky?" Her eyes roved over the shiny stainless-steel everything—the narrow vanity, the row of lights above the mirror, the compact tub with a shower.

"God, I hope so." He backed himself into the shower just enough to flick on the hot water. "But that doesn't sound like the question of a wildly impulsive woman. Losing your nerve, bad girl?"

"Hardly." She wriggled against him. "I can't wait."

Neither could he. His body reacted instantly to the movement, demanding completion, release.

Seeing the steam crawl across the steel surfaces all around them, Jackson deemed it safe to flip the switch from the faucet to the shower.

Summer practically purred when she realized the set-up.

Instead of one showerhead, Jackson's custom-made bathroom boasted five.

"I have the feeling I'm going to approve of this kind of kinky."

He just hoped she approved quickly.

"Aquarians. Water. It's a no-brainer." He shifted her in his arms to make their silhouette more compact. "Now, close you eyes and prepare yourself to get wet."

Jackson stepped over the edge of the tub, moving them into the back spray and then straight into the heart of the five-fountain deluge. Summer's head fell back, the warm water quickly working its magic on her sensitized skin.

Watching her slip into that realm of the senses gave Jackson a definite thrill. Yet somehow it seemed easier to rein in his own wants now that he could see how easy it would be to light her fire all over again.

With a renewed sense of purpose, he allowed her body to slide down over his until her feet touched the floor of the tub. Steam rolled off her body as her blond hair turned dark beneath the spray of the water. Droplets sluiced down her skin, finding secret paths along her curves he ached to trace with his tongue.

First, however, he needed to align her body in the jet stream for maximum impact. Maximum pleasure.

He twisted her shoulders, nudged her feet. Finally, he cupped her hips in his hands and swiveled them right in the path of a pulsing flow of water. The moment the torrent hit her, her knees sagged, her lips parted.

Hands reaching out to him in the downpour, Summer steadied herself against Jackson while he allowed himself to follow the droplets curving down her neck to skim her shoulder. Not wanting to interfere with the perfectly aligned streams that would help him take her to new heights, he stood behind her, positioning himself against her hips.

Ready.

He slid a hand between her thighs, exposing more of her to the relentless flow of water. Her body trembled against his as she lifted herself on her toes for one long, drawn-out moment.

After having witnessed two of Summer's passionate orgasms within the past few hours, he knew what happened next. Knew he'd found the ideal moment to ask his question.

"See me tomorrow, Summer." His lips moved beside her ear, speaking the words into her as her whole body tightened. "Let me come to the club after it closes so we can—"

On cue, she cried out the familiar words that seemed to accompany her every release.

"Yes! Yes! Oh my— Yes…"

So turned on he couldn't think straight, Jackson tossed aside his strategy, desperate to follow his own impulses this time around.

He pushed his way inside her as she came, incapable of holding back for even another minute. The waves of her release pulled him under, igniting the fire he'd scarcely managed to bank the first time around.

Yet every second he'd waited was rewarded in the backbone-melting experience of hitting that high note at the same moment. The water seemed to drum every single sensation home to him all the more, intensifying the release wracking him.

And even after the shudders ceased and their breathing quieted, they remained there, lulled by the water that had excited them only moments before. As Summer slumped back in the circle of his arms, Jackson breathed in the scent of her strawberry shampoo and hoped she wouldn't totally discount his request in the heat of the moment. He needed to see her tomorrow, had to discover how far this surreal sex would take them. He'd never met a case he couldn't win before, never met a woman he couldn't entice if he set his mind to it.

He wanted *this* woman more than he could ever remember wanting anyone, and he was willing to put every ounce of strategy necessary into making her fantasies come to life. He just hoped she would count her orgasmic cry as genuine acceptance after she came to her senses.

As he brushed back a wet lock of hair from her forehead, Jackson couldn't think of anything that would stand between him and getting what he wanted.

A STEADY, dull vibration hummed against her thigh.

Summer wanted to ignore the steady buzz, as she had probably been asleep for all of what—an hour? After she and Jackson had made love in the shower, they'd almost made it to the bed again, but stopped first for an insane encounter against the bedroom wall. At last they'd lain down, exhausted, but grinning from ear to ear.

Now she wanted nothing so much as to rest her eyes and her sore body for a few more minutes.

Unless of course, Jackson had something kinky in mind with whatever was vibrating down there....

Blinking open her eyes in the darkened room, Summer decided maybe she still had some energy left in her after all. She reached between a couple of strewn pillows and withdrew the buzzing culprit from its perch against her leg.

A cell phone.

Feeling through the darkness for Jackson, she discovered a shoulder. An arm. She smoothed her way down his chest to park the phone in front of his nose. When he didn't take it right away she felt along the length of the device until she found the switch that—

A piercing mechanical ring split the air.

Jackson reached for the phone even before he awoke fully. Did he often wake up to a ringing telephone? No doubt, his way of life differed from hers in this regard. Sure, she ran a business, but her facet of expertise involved her creativity. She didn't negotiate with vendors or search for investors the way Lainie did. Summer's work at the club remained a bit isolated and—to her way of thinking—idyllic. The day her business woke her up from a sound sleep was the day she'd cut and run.

"Taggart." His voice contained the smoky quality of sleep, an intimate note that made her think of lazy days in bed with pillow talk and shared breakfasts.

Notions that both scared and enticed her.

Her fear and longing both scattered as he bolted upright in bed.

"You've got to be fu—" He glanced up at her and seemed to rethink his choice of words. "You're kidding me."

She stared at him across the moonlit bed, this guy she'd met all of twenty-four hours ago. She would seriously consider sneaking out of the whole awkward date-turned-sexfest thing if only they weren't marooned in the middle of the Atlantic.

Besides, her body picked up on the tension in his, and she couldn't help but worry a bit over the contents of his late-night call. Make that early-morning·call, since her gut told her it was nearly dawn. Her intuition skipped along at high speed, zeroing in on definite strains of frustration in Jackson's stance, along with a healthy dose of worry and anger.

"Well, I don't care what the hell the press knows, Lucky." Jackson's gaze skittered over hers again. Then he turned his shoulder slightly. A distinct gesture of shutting her out, or perhaps simply seeking privacy. Either way, she had the impression of being willed away. "We're *not* doing the damn press conference tomorrow. I'm not in a good position to do this right now."

Unfortunately, due to their close quarters, Summer had no choice but to hear. He didn't want to have a press conference—didn't want to announce his bid for the state legislature—because he was in a *bad* position. No doubt his bad position could be related to his being with her. Surely a wild child like her wouldn't be a prudent connection for South Beach's golden boy.

It didn't take a genius or a clairvoyant to pick up

on that bit of news. Hurt knifed through her more keenly than she would have expected from a twenty-four-hour relationship. Damn it, how had she let a buttoned-up lawyer with an eye on politics get under her skin so fast?

Scooping up a twisted sheet, Summer garbed herself in cotton and stomped her way toward the stairwell so she could gather her clothes and get a grip on her wayward emotions.

She heard Jackson scramble to finish his phone call behind her as she ascended to the main deck. Why did he bother, she wondered, steam seeping from her ears as she snagged her bikini bottoms off the floor. Did he think he to try and salvage their date *now?*

Fat chance.

The time for her to be on her way back home had come and gone hours ago. She should be pleased that Jackson's dire phone call had given her an easy out from a relationship she was already enjoying a little too much.

Spying her shirt and shorts, Summer was about to drop the sheet and get dressed when Jackson sprinted up the stairwell.

With a head full of steam and a look of sheer determination etched along the strong lines of his face, he resembled a freight train ready to plow right through her.

What the—?

When she realized he had no intention of stepping around her, fear skittered up her spine. Clearly his phone call had driven him over the edge if he was about to knock her down.

Heedless of the sheet she held twisted around her

torso, Summer let go of the fabric in order to hold him off just as he reached her. Sheet sliding to her knees, she yelped when Jackson's arms banded around her body, his chest slamming into her with enough force to knock her off balance.

Luckily, he had been prepared to catch her, easily lifting her off the ground until he skidded to a stop at the back of the boat and eased her to her feet once again.

Breathless from the partial tackle, pumped full of adrenaline thanks to the scare he'd just given her and more than a little mad because she'd overstayed her welcome, Summer opened her mouth to give the man a good set down.

His hand clamped over her lips at just the same moment.

"You might not want to discuss this until you know someone has a camera trained on the boat right now."

# 7

---

*Know when to retreat.*

STRUGGLING TO SEPARATE the mental distress of
thinking they were being spied on from the physical
temptation of being plastered—naked—against Jackson Taggart's spectacular bod, Summer decided now
wouldn't be the time to fly off the handle.

She could overlook the frustration of seeing Jackson
draw some boundaries between them today in order to
cope with this new obstacle, couldn't she? Besides,
she was probably only stinging because he'd drawn
the boundaries she hadn't been able to. The man's
self-control daunted her more than a little.

His fingers slid away from her mouth. Perhaps he'd
sensed her moment of resolution, her decision to be
calm about this.

"Can we head downstairs to talk?" His quiet voice
wrapped about her like a soothing touch in the dark,
pre-dawn hour.

Unwilling to be lured in by the man's sheer mag-
netism, Summer nodded even as she took a step back
from him.

Or at least she tried to.

Jackson's arms remained unyielding around her.
"You remember the sheet you were wearing toga-style

is now down around your thighs, don't you? Unless you want to appear naked on the morning news, I think you'd let me provide my own coverage.''

Right. Naked.

Vaguely she wondered if a photograph taken in the darkness of the Atlantic would even develop properly. Then again, people did some pretty high-tech things with cameras.

''Can you reach for that sheet maybe?'' She prided herself on being unconventional, but even *she* wasn't ready to risk full-frontal nudity.

''Maybe.'' The hard wall of his chest shifted minutely as he spoke, the subtle movement sending a shiver of awareness through her. ''But you'll have to cover your…'' He glanced down at her body. ''Top half.''

Her top half immediately perked to life against him.

''Got it.'' She felt her cheeks heat when she had no business being embarrassed. ''I just need a little room to maneuver.''

He arched away by a mere inch, his lower half remaining sealed to hers. Somehow he'd managed to pull a pair of shorts on before launching himself onto the deck, but the slippery nylon left little to the imagination at this close range. Memories of the last few hours sailed through her brain even as she wrapped protective arms around her chest.

She *had* to shut off this auto-response mechanism that seemed to kick into high gear around Jackson.

Leaning down to retrieve her garb, his bare shoulder grazed her belly. ''Mission accomplished.'' He dragged the sheet up and around her, cloaking her in cotton once again. ''Let's go.''

Needing no urging, Summer picked up the clothes she'd been after in the first place and preceded him toward the stairs to the berth.

"This is your worst fear, isn't it?" The question rolled off her tongue before she dressed, before she did anything save enter the shelter of the dark hallway filled with one inflatable raft. "Being caught on camera in a compromising position is a politician's nightmare."

He steered her toward the bedroom and the tangle of blankets they'd created earlier. The sight pricked at her heart since she knew damn well they'd never crawl into a warm nest like that together again.

"It's not my worst fear, but it's definitely not good, either." He pulled a gray polo shirt out of a tiny closet in the wall and punched his fists through the armholes.

"I knew this date was a bad idea." She pressed her fingers against the ache spiraling through her temples. "I didn't need a crystal to see this coming, Jack. I just *knew* there would be repercussions to this."

"How do you figure? It's not like it was our idea to put our half-naked selves on the eleven o'clock news last night."

"Wait a minute." She sat on the bed, allowing this bit of information to roll over her. "Did you say we've already *been* on the news?" She thought they were just interested in how to prevent possible video feeds in the future.

"Hell yes, Summer. That's how I knew the camera was trained on us. There were still photos of us on the news last night." He snagged a white thermal blanket strewn over the nightstand and started folding.

"And what, pray tell, were we doing in those photos, Jack?'' Dear God, what *hadn't* they done last night? The range of options for a creative photographer was endless.

"Just kissing." He laid the blanket down on the bed to complete the last two folds, his two halves precisely equal every time. "Maybe necking. You know, like kissing times ten?"

"I'm familiar with the term." Battling a little restless energy of her own, Summer slid on her bikini bottoms underneath her toga sheet while Jackson reached for the next blanket. "But did your informant explain to you whether or not we were wearing clothes at the time?"

"We were wearing bathing suits. Or at least it looked like we were wearing bathing suits. Lucky said the photos were all taken on the deck of the boat."

All? She didn't even want to go there. "Who's Lucky?"

"My campaign manager." His words were clipped as he added a crisply folded sheet to his stack of linens.

"Oh great. Of course you already have a campaign manager. I'm sure he's a big fan of mine now." She wriggled into her shorts, then let the sheet loose to put on her bikini top. He'd seen it all before, right?

"This isn't that big a problem. People expect to see photos of me dating. I'm a guy, I'm single. No one should be too surprised to see pictures of me kissing someone. Now, if the photos had shown more of the naked frolicking, that could have been a problem. And Lucky has no reason to blame you for any of this." He turned on her to ask the question just as she tied a knot around her neck. "Jesus, woman, but you need more clothes if we're ever going to make it off this boat.''

Yanking open one of the built-in drawers under the bed, Jackson withdrew a neatly folded T-shirt and tossed it across her lap.

''Why would he blame me?'' Summer set aside his offering and pulled on her own shirt. So, maybe it soothed her ego a bit to think he wasn't totally immune. ''Maybe because I'm screwing over his candidate—literally, thank you very much—and landing you on the nightly news without your mega-starched shirts. I'm guessing this guy Lucky won't like that one bit.''

With every linen in sight now folded and stacked on the end of the bed, Jackson sat beside her. ''I realize this is awkward for you, Summer, but I promise we'll figure out a way to downplay the whole thing.''

Downplay? She turned this idea over in her mind. Visions of being shoved to the back burner in his high-profile life ran through her brain. Would she only be trotted out for posed photos at the opera with chaste kisses and formal wear? Maybe his public expected him to date more of a school-teacher type, or some social-scion kind of woman.

Neither of which could be further from her personality. No doubt this incident would be his wake-up call to put distance between them. A course of action *she* had planned to take anyway.

Then why did the notion still have the power to blindside her?

''Downplaying this might be well and good for you.'' She jammed her homemade glitter sunglasses into the tousled mess that was her hair and rose from the bed. Restless energy marched through her, desperate for an outlet. "But I don't have any intention of going quietly into that good night. I have a public profile at work here, too. And even though you might not like it, the wilder I am and the more I'm in the paper, the more people show up at the Moulin Rouge Lounge every night. My activities and the success of the club seem to go hand in hand."

"I would *never* ask you to change your lifestyle for me." His blue eyes were so earnest as he leaned one shoulder against the wall of built-in cabinetry. So frigging trustworthy. No wonder he cleaned up on the political circuit.

But Summer wasn't getting taken in by that seeming sincerity this time. She hadn't forgotten what she'd just overheard in his late-night phone call with Lucky the campaign manager. "Okay. You won't ask me to change my lifestyle, you'll just put aside your campaign ambitions until you break things off with me, right?"

His jaw dropped. Then he smacked his forehead as if he'd just remembered he could have had a V8. "How in the hell could you possibly think that?"

She poked two of her own fingers against his forehead in mild imitation of the gesture. "Because I heard you on the phone! You told this campaign guy of yours that you wouldn't do the press conference tomorrow. I believe you also mentioned you were in a bad position."

When he still looked at her as though she'd just beamed aboard from another planet, she sighed.

"I know what that means, Jack. The bad position you are in right now is all thanks to me. Something I pretty much guaranteed would happen if we went out, if you'll recall. I think we both learned a little something about dating people who are so far out of our realm of experience. It's fun but nonfunctional, wouldn't you agree?'' She scooped up her purse off the bottom step to the berth area where she'd set it many, many hours ago when their date had first begun. ''Now, if it's just the same with you, I'd like to go home. And although I had a hell of a good time with you out here, I don't think we ought to see each other again.''

THE PRONOUNCEMENT had come down with the force of a judge's gavel. Summer had ruled against him in no uncertain terms and Jackson didn't have a clue how to launch an appeal.

The sun was just beginning to rise as he secured the canvas cover on his boat. As he stored away the loose gear, he thought about their trip back to the dock outside his condo this morning. No doubt about it, the ride had sucked.

Summer had refused to debate the issue with him, preferring the view of the Atlantic to conversation. Jackson hadn't bothered sailing back, he'd simply flipped on the engines and sped them home so they could retreat to neutral corners.

But there were more rounds to go in this match, whether Summer wanted to admit it or not. She'd driven off seconds after he docked without so much as a good-morning kiss. Wham, bam, thank you, sir.

After making a quick stop at his storage area in the subterranean garage of his building, Jackson caught a cab downtown. He needed input on this situation, and it just so happened he knew where to find a semi-willing ear to hear him out on the subject.

As the cab slowed to a stop on lower Ocean Drive, Jackson spied his quarry just sliding into his regular table at a popular sidewalk café. Aidan Maddock, an FBI agent who blended into dark undercover work a little too well, had initiated the investigation into Jackson's father's misdeeds. But Jackson could hardly fault the guy who'd been his best friend since they'd roomed together as undergrads at the University of Miami.

Oddly enough, Aidan had recently hooked up with one of the other partners in Club Paradise, but Jackson had been too busy going through the hell of his father's scandal to pay much attention to his friend's new relationship. Who'd have thought the wild man would fall first?

As Jackson handed the driver a bill and stalked into the café, he told himself Aidan wouldn't be the kind of guy to hold his inattention against him, however. If he did, Jackson would know in the first ten seconds of their meeting since Aidan had never been a guy to mince words. From his Harley to the mustache-beard combo he wore like a damn rock star, Aidan made his own rules.

"You look like hell for a guy who was playing tongue hockey with a total babe on TV last night," Aidan informed him as Jackson pulled up a chair. Aidan sprawled across two seats with a coffee mug in hand, his signature ball cap hooked on a chair beside him. "Life in the public eye got you down?"

As Jackson took a seat, Aidan snitched the steaming

coffeepot from the waitress's serving cart while she was taking someone else's order.

"Shit." Jackson didn't want to discuss the news. Why couldn't they have escaped the photographers for one goddamn date? Who the hell would have followed them out into the middle of the ocean for a stupid picture? You'd think he was Ben frigging Affleck instead of a guy who just wanted to serve in a state legislator's seat. "This is big news, isn't it?"

"I won't even ruin your breakfast by showing you the *Herald*'s version." Aidan shoved his newspaper into the empty chair between them. "How the hell did you meet Summer, anyway?"

The waitress dropped Aidan's plate in front of him and removed her coffeepot from his hand with a glare. Jackson considered putting in an order for a screwdriver, heavy on the vodka. Since he really only wanted the vodka anyhow, he didn't bother.

"You've kept telling me I should drop by the club one night. I finally show up and you're nowhere to be found." He stared out over the beach. The early-morning sun cast pinks and blues over the white sand, coloring the whole strip in the pastel color scheme favored by the Art Deco District. His mind wandered back to his first glimpse of Summer and the pink braids that had decorated her hair. Hell, everything reminded him of her today. "Left to my own devices, what am I going to do besides look at women? Then *boom*—I see this goddess with lips to make a grown man weep. Next thing you know, I'm scheming for a date."

"Summer Farnsworth strikes me as a helluva wild child for a button-down guy like you." Aidan devoured his breakfast with the same no-holds-barred enthusiasm that he'd always applied to every facet of his life.

Jackson sometimes envied his friend's commitment to doing whatever the hell he wanted. Aidan had never once concerned himself with what he looked like in public or how many rules he had to bend to get his way.

Sort of like Summer, in that way. Just a hell of a lot more ugly.

"Wild? You don't know the half of it." Jackson, tipped back in his chair and let the scents of the ocean and frying bacon wash over him, distract him from thoughts of Summer. He still hyperventilated if he reflected too much on the things she'd done with him, to him...damn, but he couldn't let go of her yet.

"She's all wrong for you, Jack. You know I've got zero smarts when it comes to the men-women thing, and even *I* can see that you and Summer are diametrically opposed." He mopped up the last of his egg with a thick piece of toast. "You sure this isn't just a byproduct of the whole investigation of your father? Your old man creates a scandal that drags you through the mud so you create your own media ripple as a public way to flip him the middle finger?"

Jackson tore his gaze from the beach to stare at his friend, mouth agape. "What are you, a pop psychologist now? Shit, Aidan, this doesn't have anything do with that."

Aidan shoved aside his plate and flashed him a bug-eyed face in return. "How do I know? All I can see is that you're throwing away your career for sex. Guys like me might be willing to take a few dumb-ass risks.

But since the first day you unloaded your truckload of button-down shirts into the dorm closet—lined up by frigging sleeve length—all you've ever talked about is serving the city. Making a difference in Miami. Now I've got to wonder what you're doing to jeopardize that.''

''I wouldn't waste my time on a woman I wasn't interested in just for sex.'' If he'd only wanted a quick encounter between the sheets, he could have been with Summer that first night in the bordello suite. He leaned forward in his chair again, the front legs hitting the sidewalk with a dull thud.

''You've never wasted a second since you unpacked those starched shirts, I'll grant you that.'' Aidan signed his name on a bill beside his plate. ''Which is another strike against you hooking up with Summer, who seems like the kind of woman who would take a day off just to drink tequila sunrises on the beach or conjure funky spirits with those damn crystals of hers. Are you sure you're ready to risk a career you've worked your ass off to solidify just for—''

''It's more than sex.'' Jackson refused to listen to Aidan write off his attraction to Summer again. He didn't know what was going on between them, but he had no intention of giving it up just because it might interfere with his career.

Which—annoying as his conversation with Aidan had been—clarified a hell of a lot for him.

Aidan grinned as though he knew as much, which couldn't be possible since the guy possessed the emotional sensitivity of pond scum. ''Then stop screwing around and figure out how you can have both the high-profile political career and the high-profile wild woman.'' He pushed to his feet and clapped Jackson on the shoulder. ''But you probably ought to get dressed first. You sure as hell aren't going to accomplish anything in your swim trunks and a wrinkled T-shirt.''

Jackson told him exactly where to get off as Aidan walked out of the café. Still, he was grateful he'd at least figured out he couldn't turn his back on Summer.

Part of him had feared she'd been right on the boat when she told him he'd been putting his campaign ambitions aside until things played out with her. Tugging the basket full of coffee sweetener packets across the table, Jackson mindlessly sorted the white, pink and blue envelopes into sections while he assured himself that that wasn't the case. Maybe part of his reason for waiting to declare his campaign had been rooted in what happened between them. No doubt, she would attract loads of attention to him, and his family had already been mired in scandal.

Politics screwed up relationships, simple as that.

But he'd been delaying for weeks now because of the family scandal and the extra burden it would place on his campaign. Sure Summer complicated things, but the situation had been pretty damn complicated before she showed up.

Besides, he didn't want to be the kind of guy who put his public profile before his private life. His father had always put the former before the latter to the detriment of his whole family.

As he stuffed the creamer packages behind all the sweeteners in the square wicker basket, Jackson decided he'd need to be true to himself if he wanted to stay fulfilled by his career. No putting on a show for the camera, damn it. He drew the line at starched shirts. If the camera happened to catch him making time with a sexy blonde, that only meant the photographer had been indiscreet, not him.

Jackson was entitled to date. And he could dole out a few kisses in public, as long as they didn't get too out of control. Surely Summer could tone down the wild stuff in public and save getting naked just for him in private.

A thrilling-as-hell prospect.

From now on he would find the balance of personal and professional. Neatly divide his life into reasonable halves. His own yin and yang.

Assuming he could convince Summer to give him another chance. And assuming further that she would buy into this whole concept of order and balance.

He might have actually felt good about the plan if only he wasn't so damn certain Summer would have strewn those stupid sweetener packets into a tie-die pattern of pink and blue. No visible order. No neat stacks.

And definitely no respect for balance.

# 8

*When lost, consult the collective wisdom of your girl-friends for navigating uncharted territory.*

"EVER NOTICE how sometimes it sucks to be right?" Summer washed portobello mushrooms over the stainless-steel strainer in one of Club Paradise's three kitchens as she posed the question to one of her co-partners. She couldn't seem to shake the dark cloud that had descended on her normally sunny mood ever since she'd told Jackson she didn't want to see him again.

"No kidding." Dark-haired Giselle, the hotel's fiery executive chef, pulled her marinara-and-ricotta-cheese mixture out of the mammoth refrigerator. "I'm right all the time in my family and do you think anyone listens to me? Of course not. According to them, might equals right. So no matter how lame-brained their ideas are, they still do what they want."

This particular food preparation area produced the fare for all their catered events and serviced the meeting rooms and breakout spaces. When not in use for big events, however, it served as Giselle's personal practice arena when she wanted to try out new recipes.

And on days like today when Summer needed a temporary escape, the industrial kitchen also provided a welcome retreat. This afternoon she happened to be hiding out from all the nosy questions about her latest appearance in the papers. Everyone and their dog wanted to know more about her relationship with South Beach's most eligible bachelor.

Giselle, however, had a healthy respect for boundaries when it came to men. Ever since she'd accidentally slept with Lainie's husband long before their four-way partnership had been formed, Giselle had kept her personal relationships far, far from the club. She didn't seem to mind offering up advice on other people's relationships, however. Although Summer noticed Giselle tended to retreat a bit whenever Lainie was around.

And while Summer had always been closest to Brianne, the resort's security expert, she was finding it more difficult to talk to Brianne now that her friend had found over-the-moon happiness with her sexy FBI agent. She couldn't exactly dish about her nonexistent love life to Bri and get any sense the woman truly understood.

Besides, people in love tended to want to rope you into some big romance. The last thing Summer wanted was for Brianne to think she was doing her any favors and dropping hints to Aidan that Summer missed Jackson.

After all of eight hours.

"So the guys rule your house?" Summer passed a fat mushroom to Giselle and tried to envision what it would have been like to grow up in a house full of brothers. Maybe Summer would have been better equipped to deal with Jackson if she'd had more experience dealing with men in general. In light of her family's nomadic existence, she'd never gotten close enough to any guy to gain much insight.

Men were from Mars, women were from Venus, right? The modern maxim coincided perfectly with her view of the world. And any astrologer worth her salt knew that people who came from different ruling planets were just bound to have clashes.

"I was outnumbered four to one. Of course they ruled." Giselle stuffed the marinara mixture into one mushroom after another as Summer passed them along in random order—one fat 'shroom, one skinny, two tall ones, one broken one. The scents of pesto and vinaigrette hung in the air, comforting Summer with their hearty aroma. "And I adore them all, but they are so old-school Italian and chauvinistic, it's ridiculous. Women fall all over them because they're better looking than they have any right to be, but I'll be surprised if they ever con anyone into marriage."

Summer set aside the basket of mushrooms and moved to stir the crock full of Mediterranean seafood soup on the shiny steel gas stove. "If they can cook like you, I don't care how chauvinistic they are. Some cranky, uptight woman living on fast food would kiss the toes of any man who can make Napoleon of grilled portobello mushrooms."

Giselle snorted as she sprinkled pesto over the tray of exotic bulging fungi. "All I know is that you can't let a man run your life. I've had one hulking guy after another looking over my shoulder forever, and I'm sick of it. I'll fight my own battles, make my own mistakes, and cook my own mushrooms, thank you very much."

"There's definitely something to be said for living

on your own terms.'' Summer ladled out a bowl of soup and withdrew from the countertop area to a narrow table and chair behind Giselle. The nice thing about not being executive chef was that you could take a time-out from test preparation to really enjoy the results. Right now, Summer wanted to enjoy her soup and hope the heavenly tastes from the kitchen could seduce her senses away from memories of Jackson. ''Women have come too far to be constantly bending and changing to suit the men in their lives.''

''You said it, sister.'' After shoving her mushrooms under the broiler, Giselle yanked a bottle of house wine from a temperature-controlled vault and snagged two stemmed glasses from a rolling cart full of sterilized dishes. Settling into the chair opposite Summer at the narrow slab of butcher block, Giselle uncorked the bottle with the smooth finesse of a sommelier and poured them each a glass of the deep red drink. ''But maybe it will help to strengthen our resolve if we drink to it.''

''Sort of like a blood oath?'' A kind of pact Summer had been forced to make one too many times in the sea of funky cults her parents had joined.

Giselle rolled her eyes. No doubt she was blissfully unaware how much anxiety it produced to have to prick your own stupid finger for the sake of some bogus promise-of-the-week. Her personal squadron of Rambo big brothers probably wouldn't have let her anywhere near radical social sects. ''I'm betting a glass of the house cabernet sauvignon will be a lot more fun than splitting an artery. Why don't we toast to life on our own terms?''

She passed a glass to Summer over the steaming bowl of oysters and scallops.

"No more bending." Summer had tried compromising by going on a date that had doom and disaster written all over it. Why hadn't she listened to her instincts?

Of course, if she had, her body wouldn't have enjoyed last night's fabulous sex or this morning's pleasant exhaustion of having been thoroughly tended. Her glass hovered in midair on its way to clash with Giselle's.

Then again, her heart wouldn't currently ache with the misery of never seeing Jackson again. And no matter how much comfort food she shoveled into her mouth today, she had the feeling she wasn't going to ease that pain any time soon.

The energy of renewed commitment plowing through her veins, Summer clanked stemware with Giselle loudly enough to make her fear for the glass. "I'm with you, girlfriend. Life on our own terms."

"*Salud!*" Dark eyes glittering with quiet empathy and hurts Summer knew nothing about, Giselle drank long and deep.

And oddly, even though Summer had just sworn to forge ahead to play by her own rules, she'd broken one of her cardinal personal laws by slowly and certainly befriending her partners in the club.

She'd formed bonds with these women. Shared pieces of herself. Boldly set herself up for more broken ties if they couldn't make a go of the resort.

As long as she didn't depend on them to be there for her forever, she'd be okay. Their friendship was temporary and she was all right with that.

Jackson wielded a lot more power to do damage to her heart than these women. Getting too close to him would prove far more dangerous.

As Summer savored the flavorful bite of the cabernet, she just hoped Jackson would give her some space and not test the strength of her resolve by showing up at the resort any time soon. She had the feeling her good intentions would be easier to uphold at a distance.

With the temporary balm of friendship and a glass of wine soothing her raw emotions, Summer braced herself for another toast when the kitchen's swinging doors came flying open with a bang.

"Special report!" Brianne shouted the words as she hauled a television/VCR combo into the kitchen on a small wooden rolling cart. The wheels clattered at regular intervals as they bumped over the tile floor while an electric cord stretched out behind her into the hallway. "The network interrupted *Days of Our Lives* again, much to my dismay, but they're saying it's going to be big news from Jackson Taggart's camp."

"Do we really want to watch this?" Summer could already see the picture flipping from the local Miami anchor to a mob scene on the front steps of a building she recognized as Jackson's downtown law practice.

"Lainie gave me strict instructions to monitor the development of your involvement with Jackson in the media and any mentions of the club that might slide in, as well. Apparently she thinks your relationship with a potential legislator could be the saving grace of free publicity we've been looking for." Brianne turned up the volume, impervious to Summer's huffs of indignation.

And then Jackson's gorgeous self dominated the television screen, his spiky, sandy-colored hair and strong, angular features silencing her long enough to listen to whatever he had in the works.

He wore one of his ultrastarched shirts, the bright white providing a cool contrast to his olive-colored suit and light purple tie. Summer gave him points for the original color combination that broke the normal conservative politician mode even if not a single strand of his spiky hair dared ruffle out of place.

Brianne poured herself a splash of cabernet and leaned a hip on the table to take in the show while Giselle swiveled her chair around. Summer's three bites of lunch rumbled uneasily in her belly while she concentrated on the footage of Jackson's press conference already in progress.

"...I know some people have tried to discourage me from this race with implications that my integrity has been somehow tainted by the scandal attached to my family. But I'm here today to tell you I'm very much in the running." His piercing blue gaze connected with the camera lens and gave the impression that he spoke directly to *her*. "I will not be discouraged from the goal by a few setbacks."

Intuition told her he meant the message for her.

As much as he was telling area residents he wouldn't be discouraged, he was telling *her* that all her posturing about not getting in his way wouldn't stop him from pursuing a relationship.

A shiver skipped over her while she stomped all the intuitive perceptions that insisted he spoke of their relationship. She couldn't let him sway her, could she? Especially now that his joining the election campaign signaled one more nail in the coffin of their relationship. He'd actively chosen his work over her.

Not that she blamed him. But the knowledge still saddened her more than she'd expected.

His warm voice pressed on with just the right mixture of passion and intelligence—the kind of voice that stirred you while securing your trust. A truly seductive combination.

"Furthermore, I'm not in the race to play the conservative politics that my opponents expect. I've recently had reason to remember what makes Miami a great city is its diversity." He peered around the lobby of the law offices to make eye contact with the small throng of local journalists that undoubtedly made up his audience. "And this campaign is going to be all about embracing diversity, discovering what every sector of my constituents cares about, and figuring out how to respond thoroughly to their needs."

Summer knew first-hand the man was very good at responding to needs. No wonder he'd hardly failed at anything he'd tried. Her cheeks heated and she lied to herself it must be from the wine.

As the scene on television morphed back to the local anchor for a discussion of Miami's local political races, Lainie shoved her way through the kitchen doors, a silver pen tucked into her sleek hairdo. She smiled with open pleasure, a gesture Summer had come to realize was all too rare for the hard-nosed attorney turned CEO. "It sounds like your new man is in the race, Summer."

She didn't need intuition to hear the warning bells clanging a persistent tune. "He's not *my* man," she assured Lainie while Brianne turned down the volume on the television with the all-encompassing remote she wore on her wrist like a watch. "But I'm sure he'll do a great job if he's elected."

After all, he personified the word *strategy*. Summer would bet he'd never make a move that didn't involve careful deliberation and thorough planning.

Too bad for her.

Lainie frowned. "How could he *not* be your guy? The paper shows him devouring you like his last breath." She hunted down her own wineglass on the cart full of clean dishes then poured herself a small drink from the bottle of cabernet still on the table. "Believe me, honey, he is very much all yours."

"He *is* a hottie," Brianne chimed in, watching the muted replay of Jackson's sound bite on the video screen. "Not that you should necessarily base your love-life decisions on that."

Summer had the sense of being ganged up on. She looked to Giselle who had raised her glass to "life on their own terms" just a few minutes ago, but her friend had slipped to the other side of the kitchen and was now preoccupied with her portobello mushrooms. Yeah, normally opinionated Giselle definitely went into retreat mode whenever Lainie was around. Summer wondered if the women ever would be able to work past their differences.

Lainie clinked her glass against Summer's, which sat on the table in front of her. "But it certainly couldn't hurt to base your love-life decisions on what would be good for your business."

"Oh no." She wasn't about to let Lainie go down that road. "No way am I mixing business with—"

"Pleasure?" Lainie supplied helpfully.

"—the sheer hell of dating."

"All I'm saying is that the publicity factor attached to you and this guy will be astronomical. We're all looking for creative ways to draw attention to the resort through the media and then boom! This golden opportunity falls into your lap. Are you going to let it pass you by?" She raised a perfectly tweezed brow and sized up Summer with a narrow look. "Perhaps more to the point, are you going go let it pass by all the rest of us?"

The lead weight of responsibility dropped down around Summer's shoulders, effectively stilling her feet when all she wanted to do was run.

Lainie had missed her calling as a cult leader. The woman knew how to apply guilt with a damn skillful hand.

"I'm not promising anything," Summer warned, knowing she was toast.

Even more so because she realized she was probably using this as an excuse to do exactly what she wanted anyway—see Jackson again. A few TV sound bites and already she couldn't resist a chance to see him again. Be with him again.

Her gaze flicked over to the television screen where photos of Jackson still dominated the news coverage.

His blue eyes seemed to wink back at her. She could already feel the magnetic pull of the man tugging her back for another try.

Damn.

Score two for South Beach's golden boy.

JACKSON FOUND HIMSELF lured to Club Paradise like a moth to the neon lights. He'd waited two days since his press conference to make a move and had chosen tonight with care.

He'd given Summer a little breathing room; now it was time to press his suit. He had pithy rhetoric to throw her way—words of persuasion he'd planned in between visits to area environmentalists, food pantries and historic preservation committees. If he couldn't sway her with words, he'd operate on plan B—physical contact.

Underhanded, maybe. Strictly necessary? Okay, not really. But it was a plan whole-heartedly endorsed by a libido gone ballistic in the days without her.

After two inquiries on her whereabouts, he found himself standing outside the door of the bordello again. Apparently the room was her unwritten "home away from home" as long as no one else had reserved the space.

Strangely nervous for a man with nothing to lose, Jackson thunked his fist against his forehead a few times to get his head together, then rapped on the entrance.

Almost immediately he heard the slide of the dead bolt. The door swung open to reveal Summer dressed in pink floral jeans and a skinny purple tank top that hugged her curves. A belt that looked like a chain link fence circled her hips, the leftover metal jingling along her thigh.

Colorful braids were sporadically woven through her blond hair once again, only this time the skinny strands were light blue.

Like a breath of fresh air after three days of corporate power suits, Summer looked good enough to inhale. And no matter that Jackson had pounded his head to shake loose his tongue, the best he could come up with was a lame "Hi."

She shook her head, sending the beads in her blue braids dancing. "I've been listening to you wax poetic on television for days and the best you can come up with for me is 'hi'?"

"I've missed you." He said the first thing that came to mind.

"You're getting warmer." She smiled and capped the marker she'd been holding in one hand. "I take it you want to come in?"

"If you have a few minutes." He'd be striking out in no time if he couldn't pull himself together and make the most of the reprieve she seemed willing to grant him. He couldn't believe she was actually smiling and letting him in. How could he have missed her so much—this woman he'd spent less than twenty-four hours of his life with?

As he followed her into the sensual red haven that she'd decorated, Jackson became aware of the pungent scent of permanent marker mingling with some sort of berry-scented candle.

Unsure how long he would have her ear, however, he didn't ask what project she might be working on. Instead, he forced his eyes off the tight curve of her oh-so-fine ass and focused on his goal.

"You've been listening to some of my speeches?" If she'd tuned in at all, she'd know his core message. Would she have heard all the things he'd been trying to say between the lines?

She paused in the middle of the room and gestured toward a chair. The same seat he hadn't wanted to sit in the first time he'd come to this room.

But now, he wanted her to feel in control, to see he was willing to compromise.

Dropping onto the unapologetically feminine chaise lounge with the swirled woodwork and soft ruby cushions, Summer tucked her feet up underneath her. One bare foot stuck out to her side, the nails painted purple while a sterling silver ring wrapped around the middle toe.

"I saw your initial announcement of the campaign," she told him, swiping a kinky blond strand from one eye with the capped marker she still held. "And then I caught your address to the environmentalists along with a few sound bites on the news. You're a good public speaker."

He sensed the reserve in her words, a certain coolness that hadn't been there the other times they'd met. Spoken. Shared phenomenal sex. "I'm trying to get a certain message across."

She was a perceptive woman. Intuitive even, according to her. He wondered what she'd made of all his double meanings.

"You're trying to bring citizens together in a diverse community." She rolled the marker back and forth between her palms. The plastic tube clicked across the row of silver rings she wore, filling the momentary silence with a rhythmic beat. "It sounds like a good approach."

"I'm also trying to bring very *specific* people together, Summer." He edged forward in his chair, ready to drive home his point. "I want to heal the rifts between people who come from different backgrounds but actually share a lot of the same wants. Needs."

The heat spiked a few degrees in the bordello as his

words hung in the air between them. The fragrance of that berry candle filled his nostrils with its sweet heat, making him remember the scent of her hair and what it had felt like to roll around naked with her. To touch, taste and breathe her. Desperate for her to say something, anything, to clue him in about how she felt, Jackson found the waiting unbearable.

Finally, unable to stand another second of the clicking in an otherwise silent room, he blurted, "Are you honestly going to try and tell me you haven't heard what I've been saying to you in front of all Dade County for the last three days?"

A slow smile crawled across her face. A gleam of knowing lit her gray eyes. "I didn't want to be presumptuous."

Relief chugged through him, followed by surprise at just how much he'd been hoping for a reprieve, a second chance. He didn't know what the future held for this relationship of opposites, but knew he couldn't walk away from Summer yet, even if their liaison made waves for him politically.

He refused to live according to public expectation, and he wasn't the kind of guy to hide his true nature behind a false front. His father had tried that and look where he'd landed.

No, Jackson would at least be honest about himself. And if his relationship with Summer crashed and burned in public, he'd just find a way to deal with it.

"You're not being presumptuous." He reached for her, gripped her wrist while he set aside the marker she'd been toying with. "You're dead-on accurate. I think we could make a great team."

"But do you think so because you want to be with

me, or did you simply realize I might be the key to a grass-roots popular vote on South Beach?'' She didn't shake off his hold, but she challenged him with her gaze and seemed to see right through him.

Shit.

He couldn't deny he hadn't *thought* of that connection. But that's not why he wanted to be with her.

''I want you.'' He let her read the truth of that statement in his eyes as he joined her on the small chaise. Damn it, he knew the proof she wanted was there because he felt the want of her clear down to his toes. ''Whether you lose me some votes or win me some votes isn't the point. I'm not going to end this just because I'll be living in a glass house for the next two months. Longer, actually, should I ever want to be reelected. What I want to know is, are you with me?''

She bit her lip for a second, forcing him to hold his breath and make him worry he'd already lost her.

''I'm not going to lie to you. I have serious doubts.''

He was cut to the quick by just a handful of words. For once, he didn't know what to say. His plan B eluded him.

Shaking her head, she took a deep breath and stood. ''But never let it be said I didn't do my part to encourage harmonious diversity.''

He had no idea what she was talking about or where she was headed, but when she held out a hand to him, he took it and followed where she led.

Skirting around the bed to the back of the room, she brought them to the bathroom door, which was open just a crack. The scent of markers wafted more heavily from the small room.

"I couldn't help but be drawn in by your message, Jackson, so I went to work on a few campaign visuals I thought you might find of use." She shoved the door open and stepped aside so he could see what lay within.

Freshly painted posters, placards and handbills were scattered about the countertop and strewn over the shower curtain rod. The dominant symbol in all the pieces was the stark black-and-white symbol for yin and yang, the Chinese sign denoting balance and harmony.

A symbol he was intimately familiar with since he'd had one tattooed on his hip many moons ago.

Summer had seen, noted and transformed it into a campaign theme.

One of the placards read A Green Environment/A Growing Economy. Find Balance for the Beach. There were images of palm trees on the yin and a dollar sign on the yang. Really well-done images that hinted of a graphic-design background somewhere in Summer's past.

The art looked even more professional than what he'd been paying big bucks to an advertising firm to produce. The overall design was boldly graphic, yet artistically subtle. A perfect blend that would mean the icing on the cake for his campaign.

And Summer had created it all for him.

The thought of how much time and effort she had put into the project staggered him, made him realize she'd given a tangible part of her self with this gift.

What kind of ass would he be if he screwed up with her now that he saw through her unconventional exterior to the sensitive person beneath? No wonder she'd been hesitant to get involved. Jackson found new empathy for her relationship smarts because even as her gesture warmed him, the consequences of failure suddenly seemed much higher.

Had he thought their relationship might crash and burn in the public eye? Hell, if anything crashed and burned it just might be his heart because she had effectively stolen it with one master stroke of creative genius.

# 9

*Remain well armed at all times. Lip gloss helps.*

SUMMER HAD the distinct impression she'd committed the same relationship faux pas as a woman who hand-knits a scarf for her new boyfriend.

As Jackson towered in the bathroom doorway and struggled for words, she realized he mistakenly thought she'd spent countless hours on him when she'd actually only spent a fraction of that time.

"It's not as generous as it looks." She wanted to get that much cleared up right off the bat. Half the reason she'd made the signs in the first place had been to take their relationship to more of a professional realm. If her partners in the resort would throw her at this man, she wanted something going on between them besides the great sex that jumbled her senses and distorted her reasoning. "I had to create some mock-ups for a Club Paradise ad campaign today anyway. I thought I'd throw together a few ideas for you while I had the markers out."

He reached to slide a poster board off the double vanity sinks. "Ideas? Hell, woman, this isn't the idea stage. This looks fine-tuned and ready to slap on the front of my next podium. These are amazing."

The compliment did ridiculous things to her insides.

She'd done some of her most creative design work for the resort but there hadn't been time to really enjoy the accomplishment yet and her partners were too knee-deep in their own responsibilities to take much time to ooh and aah over her creations. If she weren't such a grounded woman, she'd swear Jackson's small praise gave her heart palpitations.

"They'd need to be recreated, of course. The circle on the yin and yang symbol was hand-drawn, and I'd want the whole thing to be more precise. But once I got the idea in my head I wanted at least to try it out on paper."

"Redone?" He stared at her as if she'd been speaking in tongues. "Summer, have you ever taken a look at what most politicians use for campaign signs? Usually it's stuff like Go Taggart or Taggart for Representative. Trust me, this is quite an eloquent improvement."

She stared down at the placard over his shoulder, reevaluating her work. The lines were clean, even if they weren't perfect. The copy strong. The visuals bold. Maybe she'd spent a bit longer on creating the pieces than she'd realized. Maybe the hour she'd thought she had spent on them had been more like a few hours, but she'd been enjoying herself and hadn't really noticed.

Glancing at her antique turquoise wristwatch, she realized it was totally possible.

God, maybe she *had* hand-knit him a scarf with her careful efforts.

She backed out of the bathroom, away from his broad shoulders and the crisp lines of his dark suit jacket. The heat of his body drew her when she knew she had to maintain some distance.

She meandered out into the bordello, then picked up her pace as she cruised past the bed. She definitely didn't need to torment herself.

"I hope you don't mind me publicizing your tattoo like that," she blurted before she really had the chance to measure her words. Mentioning a mark that could only be seen when he undressed might not be the smartest way to maintain distance. But maybe part of her had hoped to rile him. See what he'd let her get away with over the course of this campaign of his.

He wanted to bring together diverse people? Then he shouldn't mind a little outspokenness from someone who didn't know how to be conservative.

Only silence emanated from the open door of the bathroom for a moment.

Finally, he stepped out into the room again, the sign she'd made still in one hand. "It's a great symbol for what I've been trying to get across. I never made the connection, but that's exactly what I want to promote in this area. Balance. Harmony."

"And you don't mind a bit that I robbed it right off your naked body?" She pressed on when she'd meant to retreat. Clearly, her mouth would have its own way tonight.

He stared at her across the room. Which, because of the angles at which they stood, essentially meant he stared at her across the big, rose-colored satin bed. The inviting mattress decked in black lace and a soft red duvet loomed between them with all the subtlety of a porno ad.

Setting aside the sign she'd made for him, Jackson took a few steps closer.

Summer's breath caught at the sight of him closing on her. Pursuing her. Her heart slugged loudly in her own ears, the rhythm picking up pace with every inch of space that disappeared between them.

She couldn't deny that she'd missed him. Wanted him. And damn it, if they couldn't insert some modicum of shared professional strengths into their relationship, they could at least have the common ground of sex. Simple, straightforward and easy to comprehend.

Ready for the inevitable trip to that erotic bed she'd fashioned with pleasure in mind, Summer took a step forward to meet him halfway.

"Why don't I save that discussion for dinner? We can go grab something to eat in the restaurant downstairs and catch up." Maybe he caught her stunned look because he frowned midstream. "If you're not busy, that is."

Apparently he wasn't melting in his shoes to be with *her* the way she had been for him.

Fine.

She shouldn't be parceling off pieces of her heart to this man with every resounding orgasm he provided her anyway. And for all she knew, maybe his wanting to take her out in public meant he was finally prepared for anything and ready to be impulsive. A good thing, since Summer hadn't curbed her impulses or her nature since she'd broken free of the rigid cult environment at seventeen.

By being seen with one of South Beach's most visible club queens, Jackson would have the benefit of being publicly viewed as less of a stuffed shirt—something his image could surely benefit from. Summer, on the other hand would be pulling her weight with her partners by landing the resort in the papers.

The arrangement was neat and tidy and caused a tiny twinge to her heart as she longed for the simple openness of their first date on the boat.

"Dinner sounds great." Smiling brightly, she searched for her heels and hoped Jackson genuinely wanted to be a little wild tonight.

No matter that her partners had encouraged her to be seen with him—she wouldn't jump through hoops to meet a prescribed code of behavior for any man.

EVEN FOR an unconventional woman, Summer demonstrated some pretty odd behavior over dinner.

Not that Jackson minded when she read the waiter's palm, used her empty wine goblet as a crystal ball or communed telepathically with the fish in the restaurant's lobby aquarium. He simply hadn't seen her in full psychic swing before.

At least, according to Summer, that's why she spent the evening divining futures and reading stranger's auras. But as they left the restaurant for a nighttime walk down Ocean Drive, Jackson had to wonder if there might be other motivations at work.

Could this be just another Summer-ploy to push him away? Or did she really delve into psychic trances at the drop of a hat?

They attracted little attention as they slid out the dark entrance to the lounge. Nightlife on the strip didn't kick in full force for another couple of hours, although the happy-hour crowds at the outdoor bars sometimes remained heavy right up until the hard-core partiers came out at midnight.

While Summer debated which direction to take, Jackson took a deep breath, inhaling the salt breeze blowing in off the water and the unique scents of the city: the smell of tar and heated tarmac still radiating the day's warmth, the spicy scent of Caribbean food from a nearby restaurant, the exhaust from a steady stream of cars cruising Ocean Drive as they searched for parking along the crowded street. He'd been raised in a quiet, suburban corner of Coral Gables, but he'd always gravitated toward the lights, the colors, the sounds of South Beach.

The area's white sand and eclectic entertainment attracted as many celebrities as retirees these days. Countless catalogs and films were shot here with the fairy-tale setting as a background. The city had an abundance of artists and models, photographers and comics, racecar drivers and polo players. Europeans and South Americans gravitated to the area known as the American Riviera. Jamaicans, Puerto Ricans and Cubans were downright native here. The melting-pot effect translated into a wealth of culture and the assurance that an interesting person lurked on every corner.

Tonight, that person happened to be Summer Farnsworth, who wasn't European or a racecar driver, but she damn well kept him entertained. After having grown up in a family full of publicity-conscious civil servants, Jackson welcomed her unapologetic peculiarities.

"It *is* a full moon," she explained as they passed an ice-cream stand still doing great business at nine o'clock. "So that's probably why I'm receiving all these visions tonight."

They paused near an outdoor bar with a musician playing Spanish guitar for the supper crowd. Two big-breasted drag queens edged by them swinging beaded purses as they made kissy sounds at Jackson.

Summer gave them high-fives and told them she'd see them later.

"You sure it's not nervousness?" he inquired, hoping he wasn't overstepping his bounds. Hell, maybe her outspokenness had inspired him.

Her gray eyes widened. "Who me? Absolutely not. You're the one who's out with a wild woman." She swayed in a slow circle to the strains of the guitar as if to prove her point. "If anyone here is jumpy tonight, I would imagine it's you."

"Not me. But maybe that's because I know what I want." He caught her hands in midtwirl as she moved to the music. Their gazes met. Held. "Can you say the same, Summer?"

A rowdy group of drunken guys roared past them, chasing each other down the street as they hurled laughing epithets at one another. The scent of beer and sweat followed them.

Jackson didn't so much as glance back toward them as he sheltered Summer from the full-throttle charge with the breadth of his body. He watched her steadily, intrigued by this new, completely unpredictable side of her.

Still, he would swear that tonight's capriciousness stemmed from her mood—or her fears—more than any predisposal of her personality.

"I know what I want, all right." She nodded

slowly. Licked her lips. Her gaze shifted to his mouth and lingered there.

The need to kiss her buzzed through him. The need to do even more than that lurked inside him, too, the urge just barely contained so that they could have dinner. Talk. Connect on a level that wasn't horizontal.

"You do?" But if Summer had had enough conversation for one evening, Jackson could certainly be convinced to walk—no sprint—back to the hotel with her.

She smiled the wicked come-and-get-me grin of a centerfold. "Yes, I do. I want you to tell me all about that tattoo of yours."

He blinked. Rewound the conversation in his mind. Looked for what he'd missed the first time.

Damn. Damn. Damn.

Swallowing past the lust that had invaded his body with one racy look from Summer, Jackson fought his way back to some semblance of control. Intelligence.

Hell, he'd settle for simply being able to breathe again.

"I walked right into that," he finally managed, his voice rasping with bottled-up desire. He released her wrists as she smiled up at him.

She tugged him across the street toward the beach, but his ability to focus on the sights and sounds of the night had vanished. He couldn't think about a damn thing besides taking her back to the hotel suite and losing himself inside her.

Sliding her hand around the crook of his arm, she guided them over the sand and past the occasional late-night runners so they could walk along the surf. "I owed you one after you ignored the flagrant invitation of the bed in the bordello to take me out to dinner.''

"Jesus, Summer.'' She'd *owed* him one? As in, she felt like she had reason to leave his mouth watering with need? He slid off his shoes and ditched his socks, tossing them both underneath the wooden framework of an empty lifeguard's chair. "That's what women want, don't they? To be wined and dined instead of being rushed into bed?''

"Maybe sometimes. If the sex is good enough, we become cheap dates in a hurry. As in, Do Not Pass Go, Do Not Collect the Diners Club Card, and Move Straight to the Bedroom.'' The breeze off the water stirred her hair, sending a wavy strand to tease across the front of his jacket. "But since we're half a mile from the bordello with no bed in sight, why don't you tell me how you found yin and yang as a personal symbol? Then we can at least say we made a stab at meaningful conversation before we hit the sheets.''

His body stirred in response to her words. He'd never met a woman so comfortable with voicing her opinions—no veiled suggestions, no leading comments. After having grown up in a world where words were continually weighed, doctored and "spun'' to have the right effect, Jackson found Summer's total lack of artifice refreshing.

"It's not like I put a hell of a lot of thought into the tattoo thing.'' Jackson tucked Summer closer to him. She held her shoes in one hand by the long strings that had wrapped around and around her ankles, having opted to hang on to the pink short heels when he'd left his shoes behind. "I got it senior year of college on one of my last nights out with Aidan. You've met Aidan Maddock, right?''

She nodded. ''Total hottie. Brianne's really happy with her FBI stud. She's big-time in love.''

He mulled over the words, surprised at the twinge of envy ignited by the thought. Not in a million years would he have pictured Aidan the rebel seriously hooking up with someone for life before he did. Hell, Aidan hadn't had the same girlfriend for more than two weeks when they'd been in college. Yet somehow his friend had already been down the aisle once and was ready to contemplate his second trip.

Jackson's finger found a bare patch of silky skin between her tank top and her jeans. Lingered. ''We were talking one night about the future—me going to law school and him hoping to sign on with the Bureau.'' He stared down the beach that stretched on for miles, wondering if Summer had a best friend as he had had Aidan. ''And after much talk and a bottle of tequila Aidan told me he couldn't let me go to some pansy-ass law school with my starched shirts and jackets unless I got a tattoo. According to Aidan, only wusses overdosed on starch every day and I needed something—anything—to mitigate the stuffed-shirt image.''

''This is definitely sounding like a tequila-induced conversation.'' She slid her arm around his waist underneath his jacket. Even through the stiff cotton of his shirt he could feel the warmth of her palm, the cool metal of her silver rings.

''Actually, that's fairly normal conversation for Aidan. He's what you'd call a blunt speaker.'' Which was why Aidan hadn't minded informing Jackson that things would never work out between him and Summer.

Just because he spoke his mind didn't mean he knew a damn thing when it came to relationships.

"You got a tattoo because he told you to?"

"Hell, no." He smiled at the memory. "Dumb-ass that I am, I told him that I wasn't about to get a tattoo before law school unless he rode into his FBI interview on a Harley. Lo and behold, he drags me to a friend of a friend's house at two in the morning to buy a hog. By 4:00 a.m., I'm at the tattoo parlor trying to decide between a dagger piercing a rose or a darkhaired mermaid named Maria."

He could feel her laughter in the shake of her shoulders even though a noisy wave drowned out the sound. He tugged her further from the surf before their clothes were soaked, but no sooner had they taken a few steps up the beach than she pulled him back to that shifting edge where water met sand.

"But apparently you didn't go for the mermaid?" She paused, standing still to look up at him while the breeze whipped through her hair and the waves grazed her ankles.

"I think we were sobering up by then. Aidan changed his tune to tell me I'd now be a dumb-ass if I plastered a chick named Maria on my arm." Jackson stood there, amazed at the view made better because Summer was in it. The water behind her, the glittering lights of the Art Deco District behind him…both were more enticing because she was there with him. "But by then, the idea had grown on me. I wasn't leaving that parlor until I got something, anything, to remind me I wasn't just a product of my family. The yin and yang thing sort of jumped off the wall at me."

"Because you're such an Eastern religions fan?" Her smile told him she was yanking his chain.

"No. Because I had just started a quest for balance in my life, a search I still struggle for every day. It sucks to live in the spotlight with a famous family ensuring I'm known wherever I go. On the other hand, that visibility allows me to get things done that might take other politicians more time. I can put that clout and those connections to ultimate good use, but it's easier to leverage favors when I look the part." Sure, some people would find it incongruous that he would walk the beach at night in a suit. But for him, the jacket simply belonged to a uniform he wore.

He wanted her to understand, in the way few people did, why he tailored himself to public expectation. Would someone as unconventional as Summer ever see the benefit to occasionally fitting in with someone else's preconceived mold?

As her formerly open expression shuttered, Jackson began to think not.

"I have a hard time conforming to expectation," she admitted, pivoting in the soft sand to turn back the way they came. "I'd rather keep people guessing."

"Which works well for your career, too. When you think about it, we both have to adopt certain trappings to maintain believability in our roles." The breeze blew the scent of her strawberry shampoo to his nose. Her hair still danced along his jacket, a mixture of silky blond strands and baby-blue braids undulated along the lightweight wool. He would have ditched the jacket when they first hit the beach but he hadn't wanted to disrupt her arm around his waist, the silky touch of her palm through his shirt that seriously melted his starch.

"I don't play a role." She stiffened. He could sense the subtle stiffening of her shoulders beside him, the sudden rigidity of her arm against his back. "What you see is all *me*."

Her gray eyes met his in the darkness. She halted in her tracks, her hands falling away from him.

How had he managed to put her on the defensive? And why was it he could sweet talk the most frosty journalist into printing a great story about him but when it came to Summer, he couldn't seem to have a normal conversation without raising hackles all over the place.

Remembering all too vividly that he'd been in a great position to enter the hallowed sanctity of the bordello tonight only a few moments ago, Jackson sought to at least defend himself. "I just meant that while your work calls for the threads of an A-list partygoer and you play the role of club madam to the hilt, I'm in a position where I need to show up in pinstripes to blend."

Simple, right?

She shook her head, apparently not buying into his position at all. "But you're ignoring a key difference. I can choose to wear anything I want. I don't plan to 'blend' anywhere ever again."

He nodded, curious to see where she was going with this. When she only stared back at him in silence, he gathered that's all she had to say on the subject.

*Oookay.* He'd just leave unsaid the fact that her

choice to wear *anything* would never involve pinstripes and a tie. Even though he really wanted to
know why her personal fashion freedom ranked as so
important to her, Jackson realized a wise man knew
when to retreat.

"You've got me there." Reaching for her, he hoped
he could simply get on course to the hotel again and
put the night back on track. "The corset get-up you
had on the night we met blew me away. I don't know
that I've ever seen anyone play the role of bordello
babe before."

Her eyes narrowed. She crossed her arms beneath
her breasts, her pink shoes that she clutched by the
ties swinging out in an arc and nearly kicking him in
the arm. "You think I'm predictable even in my *role*
of eccentricity, don't you?" She paced in a circle
around him, then took a step closer, forcing him to
step back unless he wanted another pink leather sole
pressed to his sternum. "You think I toe the party line
of unconventionality because it's expected of me?"

He fought the instinct to put his hands in the air and
plead for surrender. Somewhere along the way he must
have stumbled into a Summer Farnsworth "hot button" and pressed it just right.

Or just wrong, in this case.

"Listen, why don't we go back to the hotel and we
can talk this out—"

"That's what you *expect* me to do, isn't it?"

Somehow, when she'd circled around him he'd
ended up next to the churning surf. As he backed up
now, the tepid water bathed his heels.

"Quite frankly, Summer, I'm not sure what to expect." He just knew his move to win her back had

somehow been seriously jeopardized and he didn't have a clue as to why. Later, he'd work on his counter-strategy. Right now, he'd settle to make it out of this alive.

Then, from the middle of left field came a smile. A full-on, drop-dead grin with the lips that had caught his attention from the start.

"That's it exactly." Dropping her shoes in the sand, she took a step back from him. "You never know quite what to expect from me, Jackson."

While he wondered how to best respond to that without causing another big scene, Summer pulled her tank top over her head…

…exposing a shiny blue bra that could almost—but not quite—pass for a swimsuit.

"What are you doing?" His politician's instincts told him he ought to turn around and see who might be watching. His instincts as a man wouldn't allow him to tear his eyes away.

"The unexpected." She flicked open the snap of her pink floral jeans.

Holy—

The woman wanted to get naked on the darkened beach while the music and laughter of the strip a mere hundred yards away still echoed in time with the crashing waves.

As much as he'd love to be a witness to whatever sizzling antics Summer had in mind, he'd be damned if he would let anyone else into the show.

She could be impulsive behind closed doors all she wanted, but her caprice was no match for his strategic planning out here in the open.

"Not on my watch you're not."

# *10*

---

*Sometimes being the hunted is as much fun as playing the hunter.*

"THOSE ARE fighting words in my book." Summer bristled at his implication despite the thrill shooting through her at his new proximity. Her fingers hovered on the zipper of her jeans. "You think you can control me or my actions?"

His body angled closer still, his broad shoulders covered in two layers of crisp clothing easily dwarfing her bare upper body. And thanks to the wonders of modern lingerie, her thin, silky bra highlighted more than it concealed, making her feel all the more exposed next to him.

"I'm not going to control your actions," Jackson assured her in that confidence-inspiring politician tone she'd come to recognize from his speeches. "I'm just going to be very, very persuasive."

His voice rolled over her with more force than any rogue wave tugging at her feet. She suspected Jackson could indeed be persuasive. Still, she couldn't bear the idea of him thinking her predictable. Worse yet, that she worked to "fit in" at the club.

Hadn't her whole life for the last ten years been about distinguishing herself as an individual?

"Sorry, Jackson." She gripped the zipper with renewed confidence. "You can be as conformist as you want, but I waved goodbye to other people's rules a long time ago. I've worked damn hard to be in control of my own life and I intend to keep it that way."

With a shift of her fingers and a wriggle of her hips, her pink jeans started a slow slide southward. She reveled in Jackson's heated stare as her clothing made the sensuous slip off her body.

Maybe she'd have a nighttime swim and let the warm water stroke her senses, caress her body. Tossing her shoes to one side, she bent to step out of her jeans when she spied Jackson stripping off his jacket.

And then his tie.

Worried, she peered over his shoulder and down the beach. "What are you doing?"

"What does it look like?" His fingers hit the buttons of his shirt before she leaped forward to stop him. "I'm joining you."

Cupping his hands in her own while her feet tangled in her pants, she restrained his busy fingers and wondered if he'd lost his mind.

"What if someone sees you?" She peered over his shoulder at his perfectly tailored jacket lying at the edge of the surf. "You can't afford to take that kind of chance."

"What if someone sees *you?*" A palpable tension radiated from him as he continued to unbutton despite her paltry restraint attempts. "There's no male fury like another guy poaching his view. The only thing that will mitigate my anger over someone else seeing you is if I'm wrapped around you like a goddamn second skin."

Summer blinked. Ran through the words in her mind again to be sure she'd really understood him properly. "You sound like a total caveman, do you know that?" Her footing slipped as the waves washed out the sand from under her feet. "Aren't you supposed to have some sort of political correctness or emotional sensitivity in the line of work you're in?"

"I'm a politician, not a saint. Read the papers, Summer. Big difference." He whipped his shirt off buff shoulders and let the thing fly like a white kite into the breeze behind him.

Summer watched it flutter and wondered if it would make it all the way up to the strip. Would some unsuspecting Ocean Drive pedestrian be at all curious when a man's dress shirt landed at her feet?

Speechless, she began seriously considering putting her clothes on and dragging this man back to her hotel room until he came to his senses.

"Besides," he reached for her, hauling her half-naked body to his and pressing her against him with too much force for political correctness. "I'm not thinking like a lawyer or a legislative candidate. I've been thinking like a man ever since you started peeling clothes off."

His heart hammered in his chest, branding her breasts with its relentless beat. His heat surrounded her, as did the pulsing energy that seemed to emanate from him ever since she'd decided to push the boundaries tonight.

Suddenly she found she didn't want to push boundaries half as much as she wanted to push Jackson Taggart to his knees and have her way with him.

But not here. Not now.

A combination of adrenaline and hormones charged through her in place of the indignation that had made her take off her clothes in the first place. She peered down the beach and saw only a handful of silhouettes meandering over the sand. A few couples too engrossed in their own worlds to notice what went on between her and Jackson. A few vagrants snoozing in rumpled lumps by the lit concrete building that housed public bathrooms in the distance.

She shivered at the contrast of an ocean breeze that suddenly felt cool compared to Jackson's hot embrace. He palmed the small of her back with one hand, his fingers straying down to rest on the waistband of her panties. Struggling to find her voice, she licked her lips. "You're starting to get the hang of living in the moment. Maybe I underestimated your ability to be impulsive."

"Do you care to renegotiate where you make your stand to show me how unpredictable you can be?" His words were even, his delivery smooth and unrushed as if he didn't suffer all the torments of lust that she did.

Must be that damnable courtroom experience that had made him so much cooler under pressure.

"I'm very much in favor of renegotiation. The sooner the better." She ran her hands restlessly over his shoulders, dying to get him alone. How had she lasted all those days since their boat trip without his touch? "Preferably conducted in a place that offers the means to get horizontal without inviting sand into my panties."

"Does that mean if I let go of you slowly, you'll be a good girl and retrieve your clothes?" He dropped a kiss in the crook of her neck, his tongue sweeping lazy, hot circles across her skin.

A smile hooked at the corner of her mouth despite the need building within. "Oh, I promise to be a very good girl for you tonight."

She could feel the shift of his lips against her throat, could hear his answering grin in his words. "It's about damn time."

He released her carefully, his fingers still grazing her hips as if to ensure she didn't make any sudden moves.

By now, she didn't care *why* he touched her as long as he didn't stop.

And he didn't.

Not when she put her clothes on. He "helped" her with that chore—doing the really useful tasks like making sure her breasts were securely tucked in her bra before she put her tank top back on.

He didn't let go of her when he put his clothes on, either—including his shirt, which they eventually found waving from a low hanging palm tree. Of course, it helped that she knotted his necktie for him, allowing his hands to roam her body at will.

In fact, Jackson kept up the physical connection between them from seaside to sidewalk and from the lobby of Club Paradise to the elevator bank.

She glanced at the clock behind the registration desk as the doors swished open to reveal an empty car. Not that they needed it since the bordello suite she favored was currently vacant and located on the main floor. "I don't have much time before I need to go to work. I wish the suite was closer and we could've—"

Jackson tugged her into the empty elevator even

though they had absolutely no need to go to another floor.

"What are we doing?" The words had barely left her lips when his mouth slanted over hers and the doors closed behind them. Hands materialized on her waist, curved over her hips, smoothed up her back to draw her body near.

"I can't wait even ten more seconds for you. We're going for a joyride." His response sounded indistinct as it was spoken against her lips, breathed over her cheek. "Just for pleasure."

Oh. *Ooh.*

The implication delighted her. Aroused her. Made her crazy for the man who could surprise her so thoroughly.

How had she ever thought him stuffy? Staid? And as far as conservative went…forget it. The man knew adventure inside and out.

He tasted sea-salty and his skin bore the scent of the ocean. Pure aphrodisiac for an Aquarian. She met his tongue with hers, craving more from the kiss. She had a vague impression of the elevator around them, the lush sienna silk moiré of the walls, the elegant gilt bench with flocked ivory-colored upholstery, and then the view faded as her eyes fell shut to absorb the impressions from her other senses.

The magnified sounds of their heavy breathing in the close quarters. The gentle lurch of the floor beneath her feet as the elevator went up. The wet slide of their mouths coupled with the urgent press of their bodies made for a kiss that had her melting, dripping, pooling all around him.

"You really shouldn't be taking chances like this,"

Summer reminded him when his hands dove beneath her shirt and he moved the heat of his mouth to cover the exposed top of her breast. "What if the doors open?"

The question surprised her since earlier in the evening she'd been playing games to see how much she could get away with in public around him. But some part of her had sensed her reading fortunes and waving her crystals at the full moon wasn't going to hurt Jackson's campaign—it would merely let her know if he planned to weigh in on her public behavior.

He hadn't.

While that knowledge comforted her, it didn't mean she wanted *him* to start taking public risks. And being caught on camera with a nipple in his mouth would definitely be more risky than palm reading.

Dropping one last kiss to her breast, he looked up at her and smiled. "I've got a plan."

He reached behind her to push the stop button on the elevator, causing the vehicle to jerk to a halt between floors.

"Maybe there are advantages to being with a strategist," she admitted, tunneling her hands beneath his shirt. "But our security techno-wiz Brianne is going to have a conniption when she sees a snafu in the system on her master control board tonight."

Jackson's hand smoothed over her belly to dip below the waistband of her damp, sandy jeans. "Good thing I only need a few minutes."

She wanted more than a few minutes. Hours alone with this man might not take the edge off tonight. But her breath stuck in her throat as his fingers delved lower still to slide inside her panties and cup her in his bare hand.

"Isn't that right, Summer?" His voice lowered, deepened, as he teased her with words and touches alike. "Aren't you close enough to coming for me that it will only take a few minutes this first time?"

His finger zeroed in on her inside her jeans. Circled the slick heat of her. She shuddered with pleasure. Rolled her hips with growing hunger.

"I don't like to put a time frame on it," she whispered back with the thready bits of control she could still gather. "No sense rushing it when—"

Her jeans slid down her thighs.

Blinking up at Jackson, she tried to guess what he would do next and couldn't. He stared down at her blue panties, his gaze so avid he surely had X-ray vision.

"There won't be any rushing. I guarantee you." He tucked his hands in the navy-colored satin and drove the scrap of fabric downward. "I just need to taste you."

Her heart kicked into overdrive along with her breathing. Did he mean…?

Jackson sank to his knees, loosening his tie as he went.

Ohmigod.

Thighs shivering in anticipation, Summer wobbled on her heels, her clothes still tangled around her feet. He steadied her as he positioned himself, his broad, tanned hands splayed across her pale skin.

And she knew she'd be lucky to last for five whole minutes. Just the sight of those hands of his on her legs, the sight of him on his knees and—

He licked her.

Not with a tentative stroke of his tongue, but with the hungered fervor of a starving man. Sweet shock waves pulsed through her, arcing out to every part of her body. She would have fallen over if he hadn't caught her tight to him with his arms.

Fingers fisting in his hair, she couldn't help but hold on to him, urge him nearer. The five o'clock shadow on his jaw scraped the delicate insides of her thighs, teasing her in the most delicious manner.

Her head tipped back with abandon and pure wanton joy. The secret vibrations that would lead to her release already tickled her insides. All it would take to fly over that ledge would be to let go mentally. Move to the realm of total sensation.

Amazed she could give herself over so quickly, so totally to this man she'd known for less than a week, Summer's thighs clenched involuntarily. Once. Twice.

Then the ultimate toe-curling tremors rocked her, washed through with the force of a tidal wave. Teetering, falling, she scrambled to grasp anything that would hold her. Her palm found the handrail on one wall of the elevator and held on for dear life.

A scream of animal pleasure tore from her throat, filling the small cabin with that raw, primal sound.

Thinking became impossible, even in the aftermath of those white-hot moments. Her brain scrambled to barely-functioning level while the rest of her body struggled to recover. Eventually her heart rate slowed, but the hot rush of blood through her veins remained a prominent sensation, especially with the increased blood flow to all the best, most exciting places.

"You mind if I help you dress?" Jackson dragged

her panties back up her trembling legs. "It's been at least ten minutes. I don't want your security friend to send out the work crews to get us started again or anything."

From the dim recesses of her brain, Summer received the message. After some effort, she managed to put together that Brianne would kick her butt if Summer wasted valuable technician time on a perfectly working elevator.

Besides, now they would go back to her suite where she could have her way with him. Granted, she didn't have much time before she needed to be downstairs to oversee the door at the Moulin Rouge Lounge. But she could be ten minutes late. Maybe half an hour late.

Even Lainie would be able to understand that some things simply distracted a woman too much to perform her job effectively. And damn it, Lainie had been the one to nudge her back toward Jackson in the first place. Could Summer help it if she developed an addiction to the man and his...talents?

She could handle this attraction to Jackson as long as she kept it in the here and now. No looking to the future, no sharing the past. Seize the moment.

Nodding, reaching for her jeans, Summer remembered where they needed to go anyway. "I want you in the bordello suite now." She fastened her damp jeans and tried not to stare at Jackson's obvious...turn-on. "First floor. Going down."

"Going down..." He echoed her words with a smile. "Is always a pleasure."

SAFE TO SAY he'd lost his mind an hour ago on the beach when Summer had started flinging off her clothes.

Jackson would have sprinted down the wide, opulent corridors of Club Paradise to get to her room now if he'd thought Summer would keep pace with him. As it stood, he contented himself with walking beside her, arm braced along her back to make sure they maintained a consistent speed.

"If I break an ankle before we get there, I'm tapping *your* insurance for the coverage, bud." She hissed the words through her teeth in a voice that mingled excitement, joy…anticipation.

"You'd never be able to argue the case since you're clearly to blame for making me hurry in the first place." Still, he tightened his hold on her waist even though he couldn't possibly slow down. "That show you put on at the beach would drive any man to desperate measures."

He didn't know what kind of switch had flipped between them out there in the warm waters of the Atlantic, but they seemed to have reached a new level of understanding. A compromise bordering on measured fearlessness—as if there were such a thing.

No doubt some rational part of his brain laughed uproariously at how ridiculous that sounded, but for the first time in forever he'd decided to indulge himself—his needs, his wants—instead of continually putting his career first. Summer's idea of living in the present made a hell of a lot of sense.

In fact, he'd already enjoyed it so much he'd found nirvana in a hotel elevator. Damned if he wasn't a true convert.

"Desperate measures?" She glided to a stop outside

the doorway to the bordello suite, the electronic key-card already in her palm. "Maybe I ought to be the judge on that particular case, counselor. I'd be very interested in hearing about your level of desperation."

Filching the card from her hand, he stuffed it into the slot and shoved open the door at the earliest possible second. He held it wide with one hand while nudging Summer inside with the other.

"Funny you should ask." His heart slugged a thick, slow-motion rhythm in his chest as he looked at her. He still couldn't believe he'd talked her into going out with him in the first place. That she continued to see him despite his high profile in the community. "I was just about to tell you in no uncertain terms how much you're tormenting me tonight."

Her gray eyes widened in mock innocence, her lips forming a delectable pout. "Oh really? I thought it was me who was enduring all the torment. Or did you forget about the encounter in the elevator?"

She sashayed her way inside the room on her pink, lace-up heels as if she had all the time in the world. Her walk could only have been intended to snag his eye, and did it ever. His gaze glued itself to her swinging hips and the narrow band of waist exposed by her short tank top.

"I remember it perfectly." Flinging his jacket aside as the door swung closed behind them, Jackson unbuttoned his shirt and followed in her footsteps. "My memory is all the more enhanced since I still have the taste of you on my lips."

Her sashay faltered as she reached the sitting area. She pivoted on her heel to peer at him.

"Is that so?" The smoky tones of her breathless

reply nearly undid him. He finished with his buttons, his shirt sliding off his shoulders along with his unfastened tie.

He remembered her fantasy about being overpowered as she stood there in the middle of the room looking delicate and vulnerable on the outside when he knew she was hot and bothered on the inside.

But his own brand of intuition told him it wasn't quite time for that. He needed to gain more of her trust, a trust he would build on tonight.

Even though he wasn't—damn it all—looking toward the future. He would enjoy this moment.

"Yeah, that's so." He licked his lips to remind himself what it had been like to taste her, touch her, ignore everything else around them. Damn but he needed to do that more often. All of the above, in fact. "And I would argue that you *haven't* been tormented since— if I'm remembering correctly—you've already taken flight once tonight while I seem to be dying for that same opportunity."

Summer's gaze lowered to his trousers. Lingered. His erection severely compromised his zipper.

"So I see." She kicked off her heels and stepped closer until mere inches separated them. "Lucky for you, the Mistress of the Bordello knows exactly how to handle these matters."

"Uh, Summer? I hate to break it to you, but I don't know how much 'handling' I'm going to be able to endure. A guy's got his limits, you know. Tonight might be testing mine."

"Then maybe we'd better skip the formalities?" Her arch expression told him she knew what she was about. With an eat-your-heart-out pout of her perfect lips she reached for the hem of her tank top and edged it up over her head.

Somewhere within him, an engine revved. He could practically hear his internal motor growling with an energy he could no longer restrain. He reached for her jeans, unable to wait for the striptease.

"No formalities." He tugged the pink floral denim down her thighs. "No handling." Reaching for his belt buckle, he kept his gaze steady on her as he undressed the rest of the way. Then he reeled her in close to him again, his hands intent on divesting her of the last scraps of satin clinging to her beautiful body. "And not a damn thing between you and me."

She gasped as he curved his hands around her bottom, settled her hips against his for full impact.

That lone needy noise only fueled the fire within.

"What do you say, Summer? Do we need to do anything outrageous or does the Mistress of the Bordello occasionally approve of straightforward, back-against-the-wall, drive-you-out-of-your-mind sex?"

# *11*

---

*Losing a battle can also increase the manhunter's powers.*

SUMMER VAGUELY WONDERED how many women Jackson Taggart had undressed in his life for him to have acquired such lightning-fast hands with her lingerie. Still, she appreciated the benefits of those talented fingers as he backed her up to one wall, pursuing her until she had no room left to run.

Not that she was running, precisely. More like enjoying every second of Jackson's seductive chase.

The lush softness of shirred velvet on the walls met her bare bottom as she stopped. A split second later, the rock-solid length of Jackson met her front, pinning her in place.

"The Mistress of the Bordello has never needed any extraneous toys or…" She cast a quick glance downward. "…tools to enjoy sex. My only requirement is a prophylactic and a willing stud."

Jackson flashed her a glimpse of her first request in the palm of his hand before he tore open the packet. "I think I've got both of those things covered. Although you sure as hell better want more than just a willing stud inside you."

"Is that right?" Her knees dissolved beneath her as

she turned boneless with wanting. If he didn't take her soon she would climb the wall.

"The correct response would have been that you want *me*." Sheathed and very ready, he nudged her thighs apart. "Only me."

He stretched one long arm down the back of her thigh and then drew her leg up to encircle his waist. Steadying her hips, he lifted her against the wall, her spine sliding against thick velvet as she wrapped her other leg around him.

Positioned perfectly, she couldn't stand the wait, couldn't bear the need another second. She arched her back, raised her hips and sank down the length of him in one slick stroke.

Jackson's groan echoed the one she held inside her chest. Part of her brain still somersaulted with the thought that he'd told her to want him and *only* him. That small phrase added a new dimension to this joining, a sense of connection that made her want to forget about all the reasons they didn't add up together.

"Yes," she sighed, whether in agreement to his words or in rapturous encouragement of his touch, she couldn't be sure.

She only knew she wanted him to continue doing everything he was doing to her right this second. The deep thrusting of his hips, the flexing of his arm around her waist, the lick of his tongue over pebbled nipples. Everything inside her shouted yes to this man's caress, his unequivocal possession of her body.

"Hold on to me." His hoarse voice whispered over her ear, her only preparation for his sudden grip on her thighs before he walked them across the room, never breaking their intimate contact.

Who needed to hold on when a powerful man held her in his arms? Instead, she opted to rain kisses over his face and down the rough edge of his jaw. The warmth of her breath heightened the faded scent of clean aftershave.

Her lips had almost reached his mouth when she fell backward onto the red satin of the duvet covering the bordello's showpiece bed. She'd designed the room so carefully, hardly daring to hope she might one day enjoy the sensual details she'd agonized over.

Now, the cool satin sent shivers over already sensitized skin, the skittery sensations mingling with the hot, edgy need inside her.

She caught a glimpse of Jackson poised above her as he remained standing at the edge of the bed, their bodies still deliciously joined. He could have been a Greek god, every muscle tensed and clearly delineated to her hungry eye. Sheer masculine perfection, Jackson made her mouth water.

And that wasn't the only place where her juices were currently flowing.

She could have hit an all-time orgasmic high just watching him tower over her from that angle. But when he bent to cradle her body in one arm and to stroke her bare skin with his fingertips, Summer feared she would expire from the liquid tenderness flooding through her.

Shutting her eyes against an intimacy she wasn't ready to face, Summer struggled to concentrate on the knot of silken tension tightening inside her. A simple task given that Jackson's fingers skimmed her slick heat, circled the source of that tension, and teased her to new heights.

Caught in a web of pleasure, she cried out when he hit that magic flashpoint, sensations rocking her whole body with the force of her gratification.

She felt him move inside her, certain she would explode from the exquisite friction. Instead he succumbed to the heat, echoing her release with his own.

Through the veil of heavy breathing and hoarse shouts, Summer could have sworn she thought she heard him whisper the words that had been chasing around her brain.

Only me.

But then, that simply could have been wishful thinking.

WHEN SUMMER'S clock radio alarm crooned the second time, Jackson knew he'd have to let her go. Late for work already, she had ignored the first blare of blues music from the bedside table.

Trouble was, he didn't want to release her. Limbs still entwined from sex that left him speechless, they lay cradled in red satin. His heart rate had barely begun to return to normal and his brain had begun to wonder how he could have Summer in his life and think only about the here and now.

They'd been back together for all of a day and already he had to ward off thoughts of a future together. She'd lent her creative talents to helping him put together campaign signs, even going so far as to come up with a great new slogan for him. She'd curbed her impulses on the beach for his sake, waiting until they'd found the relative privacy of the elevator to go wild with him. How could he *not* think about what it might be like to wake up next to this woman in the days, weeks—maybe even months—ahead?

She inspired a possessive streak he hadn't even known existed.

Reaching for the alarm clock, Summer reset it. Again.

"Who cares if I never make Employee of the Month," she grumbled, shoving the lightweight radio back on the nightstand. "I'm an *owner,* damn it."

Undeniable warmth kicked through him as she resumed her position curled against his side, blond hair streaming over his chest like a bonus blanket. Much as he tried to tell himself that warmth was an automatic male sexual response to having a naked woman glued to his side, he knew damn well there was more at work here.

"You're entitled to some downtime," he assured her, tugging the red satin more snugly around her shoulders. "As ambiance coordinator for the resort, you did all the decorating and design work for the revamped rooms, right?"

He recalled that Club Paradise used to be the tackiest couple's resort in southern Florida. Thanks to the efforts of the new ownership, the hotel had a sleek new approach as a lush playground for singles.

"Every carpet and wall treatment, every tile and linen—it's all mine. Excuse me if I blast my own horn a bit, but I still can't believe it when I look at how it came together. I'd never taken on such a big project for any job before." Her breath fanned over his chest while she spoke.

He tipped her chin up to meet his gaze. "You must have worked nonstop for months. And for a woman who doesn't mind drawing attention to herself in the media, I have to say I'm surprised at how little you ever tout your own work.''

If *he'd* created the unique atmosphere of the resort, he'd be shouting the success to every design publication in the U.S. Of course, Aidan would roast him big-time if he went into decorating, but still…Jackson had never been one to downplay his accomplishments.

Summer, however, seemed to harbor an unexpected modesty when it came to her career.

After giving a half-hearted shrug, she repositioned herself on the pillow beside him, her movements clipped, tense. ''It's not that I don't take pride in the work. I just never know how long my dedication to a cause will last. I figure why bother shouting my good news from the mountaintops when I might get bored with the endeavor next week and take up flamenco dancing or bongo playing.''

''First of all, if you take up flamenco dancing, I will hunt you down to see you in the outfit.''

She grinned. Some of the tension in her shoulders eased, just as he'd hoped.

''Second,'' he continued, stroking a long strand of hair from her cheek, ''do you really think you could walk away from Club Paradise after having poured so much of your heart and soul into this place?''

Her personality had been etched in every outrageous line of the bordello suite. How could she leave that much of herself behind?

Worse, was she seriously thinking about shipping out of Miami Beach any time soon? The pang twisting in his chest at the idea of her leaving surprised him.

''I don't have any plans to go tomorrow or anything, but traditionally, that's how I've worked in the past. I have a big burst of productivity and I win accolades all over the place. And then…''

"You ditch?"

"I get bored.'' Her voice held a defensive note as she toyed with the black-lace edge of the satin comforter.

"So have you left a trail of five-star hotels and sexy room decor in your wake?'' He really hoped that damn alarm clock wouldn't be blaring again too soon. The more he stared into Summer's gray eyes, the more he realized he wanted to know about her.

"Hardly. Club Paradise was my first chance to design on a big scale. I've dabbled a lot up until now.'' She propped her hand on his elbow. Beneath the comforter they'd wrapped themselves in, her instep traced circles along his calf.

The warmth of the gesture lulled him. Made him wonder when was the last time he'd been with a woman who didn't run straight to the bathroom after sex to reapply lipstick and comb her hair.

"Dabbled?"

"Everything from pizza delivery to gymnastics coach. I took a cheerleading squad to the national finals one year.'' She punched the air with her fist in a classic cheerleading move, then did a snappy little nod that send her hair whipping around her head. He could almost hear the marching band music in the background. "Want to see me bring it on?"

"A cheerleader? I sort of pictured you as the kind of woman who always took the road less traveled, and all this time you were a cheerleader?'' He couldn't envision her with her glitter sunglasses and her blue braids fitting into the most notoriously conformist group on any high-school campus.

"Not when I was in school. I took it up later in life after—honest to God—playing trombone in a marching band at college. I sort of envied all those cool moves the cheerleaders made, so I worked out with the team a little, just for fun. Two years later I saw a position for coaching a cheer team a few states to the north of me and I took the girls to the big show. It was a total trip."

"What you're telling me is you have the Midas touch."

"The devil's own luck, according to my mother."

Again, she gave the shrug. Didn't she realize how charmed her life would sound to most people?

"More like a massive assortment of talents. You're a Renaissance woman, Summer." But he wanted to get back to something that had piqued his curiosity earlier. "With all that success—how do you end up getting bored?"

She wriggled as if the question made her uncomfortable. Her gaze darted around the room.

Taking a deep breath, she looked ready to take a stab at an answer when the alarm on the nightstand went ballistic again.

"See that? Saved by the bell." Scrambling to turn off the noise, Summer fled the bed and the conversation. She waved the clock radio with one hand, a grin playing with her lips. "I have the devil's own luck."

As she disappeared into the bathroom to get ready for work, Jackson wondered if she was really as lucky as she thought.

Any woman who needed to run so far, so often must

have reasons. Hadn't anyone ever given her grounds to stay in one place?

Not that he'd been thinking about enticing her to stick around South Beach. Hell, who was he kidding? His brain already had skipped ahead to solve that particular puzzle.

Damn.

One day back in bed with Summer and he'd forgotten about his live-in-the-moment credo. Too busy making plans and strategizing the hell out of every last piece of happiness he stumbled across.

Lucky for him, it wasn't too late to start using his head. He had to campaign tomorrow and he needed to be awake at 5:00 a.m. No sense hanging out at the club all night trying to figure out more clues as to what made Summer Farnsworth tick.

For once, he'd take a page from her book and cut and run. She probably didn't expect him to stick around anyway since she had to leave for work. Scribbling a note on the pad of paper beside the bed, Jackson ignored the clench in his chest as he searched for his pants.

SUMMER POUNDED her pillow with both fists. For one thing, she couldn't get back to sleep the next morning after the sounds of a cranked car stereo down on the street woke her up. For another, she was still pissed Jackson had skated out the door on her last night while she showered.

Damn the man.

She flopped to the other side of the bed, twisting the sheets hopelessly around her feet. In the past, she'd always enjoyed her vagabond lifestyle and sleeping in different rooms of the hotel every night. But after her talk with Jackson, her rootless existence felt less exciting and more…*pathetic?*

Surely not. Closing her eyes against the thin stream of sunlight determined to blink through the one slit between heavy drapes, Summer reminded herself she moved around a lot because she wanted to, not because she had to. An important distinction that made her life a lot different now from when her folks had carted her around the country on *their* time schedule.

She made her own rules now.

Didn't she? Of course, talking about her stint as a cheerleading coach forced her to remember that she'd left that gig because she'd been tempted to have an affair with the gym teacher. Since that seemed like a bad example to set for her girls, she'd resigned. Found herself a job a few states away. The move had seemed to make perfect sense at the time, but she was beginning to realize the rest of the world didn't live this way.

Most people stayed and ironed out their problems. In fact, some people who didn't realize how much she enjoyed being a free spirit might actually draw the conclusion that she was a first-class coward.

Bolting upright in her bed she wondered if that's how Jackson viewed her. Because it would really annoy her to think so.

Giving in to the inevitable, Summer pried herself out of bed to dress for the day. She had four thousand things on the agenda, not the least of which was a follow-up with *Wanderlust* magazine to try and finagle a feature on Club Paradise. She didn't mind admitting *that* particular thought scared her.

Jackson might have been wrong about her having the Midas touch—though the compliment had definitely made her smile—but he'd been dead-on when he'd guessed that she wasn't the sort of person to tout her own work. And calling the most upscale travel magazine in the states and asking them to feature Club Paradise because of its unique designs—*her* unique designs—definitely smacked of bragging.

But Lainie had laid down the law, and even though Summer found Lainie's management style a bit brusque at times, she admitted the woman had a head for business. She trusted Lainie wouldn't be pushing all of them so hard to garner whatever publicity possible if they weren't financially desperate for the attention.

Unfastening the blue braids that she'd worn yesterday from her hair, Summer thought back to how much Lainie had impressed her when Summer had first come to the resort. At the time, Summer had only been concerned with learning the ropes of her position as activity director from one of the lesser big shots at the hotel.

That two-timing louse who'd barely held his own in bed anyway…ha! She pulled a brush through her hair and slid on a new coat of lipstick, remembering the slick restaurant manager and security coordinator who'd hired her. He'd quickly become her on-again, off-again boyfriend until he'd bounced out of town along with the rest of his embezzling friends, leaving their women behind along with their hotel.

Morons.

They'd been too shortsighted to see how much of a moneymaker the resort could be with the right guidance. And sure, maybe the fact that Summer had been dumped for the first time in her life had something to do with the fact that she'd been so determined to stay on at Club Paradise and turn it into a top-notch property. What woman scorned didn't get off on a few ''in your face'' turnabout tactics?

But since then, she'd learned to love South Beach and find real fulfillment in her work. Come to think of it, staying on at Club Paradise might have been the first time she'd remained grounded during a period of turmoil in her entire life.

Interesting. A clue that she wouldn't get bored in South Beach any time soon? Maybe. As long as Jackson Taggart didn't scare her off with unrealistic demands, perhaps she would continue her stint here as ambiance director for a long time to come.

She sidled into a skinny T-shirt and a pair of khaki overall shorts thinking if his running out of her bed last night were any indication, the man probably had no intention of demanding a damn thing of her.

Contrary female that she was, for some reason that really bothered her even while she told herself it was a good thing. Probably because she felt way too much for the man when she'd only just met him.

But honestly, had any man ever compromised with her before the way Jackson had? She told Mr. Conservative she liked impulsiveness, and he promptly sent her into orgasmic bliss in an elevator car. She said she needed to be her own person and he didn't so much as bat an eyelash when she'd started reading palms in public.

Oddly, his effort to make a few concessions toward her had encouraged her to compromise right back.

Otherwise, she never would have been swayed to quit her skinny-dipping attempt last night on the beach. But somehow Jackson's husky plea that she save the show for him had tugged at her heart as much as her hormones. She'd been so hot for him by the time they got back to the hotel she'd melted all over him before they even found a room.

Dressed and ready to take on the day, Summer blew a kiss to the image of herself in the mirror. After all, she didn't look half bad for a woman whose date had sprinted out of her bed last night. In fact, she looked like a woman who'd finally learned how to strike the right balance between having a gorgeous man in her life…a man with a sexy tattoo, no less…and maintaining her own identity at the same time. She'd found a man who was willing to compromise, a man who wouldn't look toward the future or pry into her past.

Seemed like a damn good reason to celebrate.

Scooping her room key off the coffee table in the sitting area along with her purse, Summer headed for the door humming a little tune. Maybe she'd call Jackson today and see if he wanted to hang out in between his political appearances.

If he hadn't been scared off by the idea that she cut and run on a regular basis, what could possibly scare him off now?

She pulled open the door, full of new hope for a manageable relationship for the first time in forever.

Only to find Giselle and Brianne lurking in the hallway.

Nearly stumbling over a small room-service cart, Summer took a step back, the door behind her thudding against her bottom as she did.

Brianne and Giselle exchanged cryptic looks before Brianne hit a few buttons on the techno-gizmo remote thing she wore on her wrist and Giselle smiled a super-fakey Hostess Barbie smile. "Would you like some breakfast? We thought we'd all eat together this morning."

Concern—no, make that panic—coursed through Summer at being double-teamed by her co-owners so early in the day. Sure it was almost noon, but for a group that worked well into the wee hours at a nightclub, this was the equivalent of the crack of dawn.

"What happened?" Her instincts flared to high alert. "Is the resort sinking in a sea of red ink? Is the bank ready to foreclose?"

"Of course not!" Giselle rushed to reassure her even as she bustled her rolling cart complete with coffee, pastries and granola inside the bordello suite. "We just thought we'd have a meeting in a more comfortable setting."

"Like my messy room?" She didn't buy it for a minute. Glancing toward Brianne, Summer started to panic just a little as she watched Bri pull the door closed behind them. "Come on Bri. What gives?"

"Lainie will be here in a minute," Brianne supplied, following the food cart with her long, cool stride. "We just needed to talk."

"Is the club in trouble?" She had to know that much, damn it. The resort had become her whole life over the last eight months.

Again there was a secretive exchange of looks between the other people in the room.

Summer stamped her feet, ready to explode. "If

there is a problem, you damn well better let me in
on it.''

Just as she spat the sentence out, the lock snicked
in the door and Lainie joined them, a newspaper rolled
under one arm.

A newspaper.

The back of Summer's neck prickled with a flash
of premonition. Her heart rate kicked up a panicky
notch as she recalled the last time she'd been in the
paper.

Nearly naked. With Jackson.

Lainie took quick, efficient steps to meet them in
the middle of the room where they all congregated
around the sitting area. "Actually, there is a problem,
Summer. But it doesn't have anything to do with the
club." She joined the rampant exchange of enigmatic
looks before she blurted out the rest. "It's of a more
personal nature."

From the depths of her purse still clutched in one
hand, Summer heard her cell phone ring.

And ring.

Her nerves stretched thin along with her patience.
"Somebody please tell me what the hell is going on."
She fished in her purse to put an end to the ringing.

"Wait." Brianne gripped the purse before Summer
found the phone. "It's probably Jackson and you
might want to hear this from us first."

Lainie tugged a tabloid sheet out from under her
arm while Summer backed into the loveseat. While her
heart thumped louder in her ears, she recognized Giselle's hands on her arm guiding her down to an up-
holstered cushion.

The phone quit ringing.

Laying out the newsprint on the coffee table, Lainie shoved aside a stack of furniture catalogs. "The South Beach arts weekly published a crappy, invasive piece about your past."

"It might not even be true," Giselle hastened to explain as Summer's eyes landed on a photo spread of her past, a montage of memories she'd rather forget splashed all over the center pages. "But we didn't know enough about where you came from to know if this was all lies or if..."

Summer's gaze focused on the picture in the middle of the piece. She was marching in a demonstration somewhere in the northwest when she was about fifteen or sixteen years old, but already she looked all of twenty-one. The participants were all dressed in black and each carried a white candle in one hand and a long quill in the other. It had been the summer they joined the Secret Society of Automatic Writers.

Not that there had been anything in the least secretive about them after they'd paraded up and down a local thoroughfare to protest the treatment of exotic birds.

But what caught her eye in the photo didn't have anything to do with quills or birds or candle rituals.

As her gaze trailed over the hastily compiled life retrospective of Summer Farnsworth, the same thing caught her eye in the photo of her with her parents being arrested for disorderly conduct at a political demonstration. And the photo of the new inductees into the Upstate Wyoming High Order of Druids. Also the not very flattering picture of her with her new braces alongside her folks at a Shinto celebration in Arizona.

"It's true," Summer admitted, filling in the silence that had probably grown a bit awkward for her friends. "I don't think anyone would ever think to make up something like the Upstate Wyoming High Order of Druids, do you? The truth is usually a hell of a lot less believable than fiction."

And in this case, the new truth unveiled to her adult eyes possessed a healing power she hadn't ever expected to find. Because, unlike her memory that had recalled a childhood being an outcast while her parents easily blended with every new cult they had ever joined, the pictures told a different story.

In picture after picture, her whole family unit— mother, father, Summer—stood off to the side. Apart. Outcast.

Not just her.

Lainie sank to the seat on the other side of Summer while her perfectly manicured hand slid around Summer's arm in a serious grip. "Look. I know I've been encouraging PR at any price for the sake of the hotel, but this is bullshit. Not a single one of us would want our pasts dragged out in the open like this and we're all willing to go to bat for you here. We'll pull our ads from this rag for starters—"

"I appreciate the offer." In fact, the offer meant the world to her, especially coming from Lainie. The woman had never made friends idly. When Summer had first met the partner with the largest share of stock in Club Paradise she'd been intimidated by Lainie and her take-no-crap attitude. A year ago, Lainie had still been married to Robert Flynn, one of the resort's big shots along with fellow Rat Packer Melvin Baxter. For all her intuitiveness, Summer had never been able to fathom how a brilliant, self-confident attorney like Lainie had married an obvious player like Robert. "But I can't let you do that. I can handle this."

As uncomfortable as she might be with hanging her past out to dry in front of all of South Beach—and Jackson, and all of Jackson's voters—Summer couldn't regret the overblown feature.

Brianne dropped to the settee across from them. "You don't have to take it quietly. We've all agreed this crosses a line."

Summer smiled, more pleased than they could guess at their quick defense. "Honestly. It's not a problem. My past is as crazy as my present. So what if the world now knows I've taken blood vows to uphold the laws of three dozen different secret societies in my lifetime? This is South Beach. That's supposed to be okay here. That's why I love it."

Giselle whistled under her breath.

Brianne smiled.

Lainie shook her head. "You're *fine* with this? You could have a slander case in the making. Did you read any of the article, Summer? This moron reporter suggests you might still be wanted in two states."

"For what? Chaining myself to a birdcage when I was twelve? Trust me, if I could pass a fingerprint test three years ago to coach a high-school sport, you can bet my record is clean as a whistle. The moron reporter obviously just wanted to draw stupid conclusions because he had nothing concrete." Other than some really interesting photos of her past which proved she wasn't the only outcast in the family.

Damnation. No wonder her parents hadn't remained anywhere for more than five months at a time. They were even more clueless than she was about how to fit in.

But Summer might actually be figuring it out. She had three friends sitting around her right now trying to protect her sorry butt from malicious gossip.

And she had a phone ringing in her purse from a man trying to...what?

Protect her sorry butt, or his?

She wasn't sure which option scared her more.

# *12*

---

*A beast may be captured, but never tamed.*

"THE TIME has come to cover your ass, Jack." Lucky Adams rifled through the kitchen cabinets in Jackson's condo, banging one wooden veneer door after another in a mad search for coffee mugs while they brainstormed how to get around the latest road bump in the election campaign. "You wanted to jump into this race at the bitter end, which means you've got very little time to form public opinion. If you want that opinion to be positive, you need to distance yourself from stuff like Club Madam Exposes Liberal Roots."

Jackson yanked open the pantry to point out the cups. Why the hell wouldn't Summer answer her phone? He was going to lose his mind if he had to fend off anymore of Lucky's worries. He had enough of his own to face without easing someone else's. "I'm running on the independent ticket. What do I care if she's got a liberal side?"

"A liberal side?" Lucky slammed the mugs to the counter and wrenched the steaming pot out of the coffee machine. Sleeves rolled up and his normally spiky hair now totally standing on end, Lucky scrubbed a hand over his jaw. "Who the hell has even heard of the High Order of Druids? They're so out there they're off the political maps. I think they elect a governing body of trees, right? The redwood runs against the birch for Forest Council or something?''

"You're being close-minded.'' Though even Jackson wondered how Summer's parents could have involved her in such a mishmash of ideologies. No surprise Summer was the most unique female he'd ever met. She'd come from the single most bizarre background he could imagine. "And to set the record straight, I have no intention of distancing myself from Summer unless…''

Lucky put the coffeepot down so fast he sloshed Colombian dark roast all over the cabinet. "Unless what?''

Jackson spun the paper towel dispenser and ripped off enough to clean up the mess. Damned if his whole life hadn't been about cleaning up other people's messes lately. His father's. His family's. Lucky's.

He wouldn't add Summer to that list even though his relationship with her had caused him a fair amount of trouble. He was the one running for office. If Summer hadn't possessed the bad luck to date a politician, none of this would be happening to her now.

"I won't distance myself from her unless that's what she wants.'' He sponged up the coffee and dried off the counter, hoping like hell it didn't come to that. But would Summer even recognize the mess this so-called feature would cause for her? Damn it, knowing Summer, lured by a little controversy, she'd probably only wade deeper into the fray.

And that wouldn't be good for her or for the latest career she seemed to really, really enjoy. How could he in good conscience let her get raked over the coals because of him?

Lucky sighed as he plunked into a rich cherrywood chair pulled up to a granite countertop. Jackson still didn't understand how his mother could decorate his damn apartment with *Better Homes and Garden* perfection, yet he couldn't find a travel mug to save his life.

"Somehow I doubt she'll want to back off now," Lucky prodded, as if determined to annoy the hell out of Jackson today. "Has it ever occurred to you she might be in this relationship for the publicity?"

Jackson wondered what his chances of winning the election would be if he fired this guy here and now. "Has it ever occurred to you this might be just as much a pain in the ass for her as it is for us?"

Not particularly wanting to hear Lucky's answer to that question, Jackson picked up his phone and dialed Summer's number again.

No answer.

"I'm heading over there." He needed to talk to Summer before this thing got too far out of hand. Before she buried herself deeper by talking to the media.

Snagging one last gulp of caffeine, he reached for his keys on the top of the microwave.

Lucky rose to put a restraining hand on Jackson's arm. "You may want to tell her that this kind of questionable publicity might help their nightclub, but it's sure as hell not going to help business at that ritzy resort hotel they're running over there."

As if Summer wanted this guy's advice. Although he probably had a valid point.

"You know what? I think she'll manage just fine

without your guidance, but thanks anyway.'' Jackson shook off his arm and headed for the door. "And if we're going to keep working together on this, you need to keep your suggestions focused on my campaign and not my personal life."

The heavy door was already closing behind him when Lucky's voice drifted down the hallway in his wake. "Shit, Jack. Hasn't anyone told you that you can't separate the two in politics?"

SUMMER PEELED another onion and tried not to cry as the scent wafted around her face, burning her eyes. It's not like she was hiding out in the back corner of the kitchen or anything. She genuinely wanted to help Giselle get ready for tonight's dinner. They'd received double the number of usual dinner reservations already, surely thanks to the Club Madam article.

Of course, Lainie hadn't mentioned it, but after a quick scan of the reservation log for the hotel, Summer had realized there had also been two room cancellations today. And if the Miami *Herald* picked up the local story, the backlash would be ten times worse. Local patrons might want to have dinner at Club Paradise to check out the gossip, but they didn't necessarily want to mire themselves in the controversy by staying in the hotel for a long weekend.

Giselle delivered another batch of onions to the countertop beside Summer's cutting board. "You okay? You want me to send Renzo out to kick that reporter's ass?"

Peering over her shoulder at one of Giselle's towering big brothers as he monitored the progress of garlic bread in a wall full of brick ovens, Summer decided the guy looked ready for the job. With dark hair and olive skin, he had Hot Italian Stud written all over him—if she had been into that type. Summer seemed to have caught a case of vicious attraction to sandy-haired politicians.

Renzo canted closer, possibly lured by the discussion of an ass-kicking. "She's not kidding. Nico and me have been looking for a target for butt-whooping ever since Giselle started working this gig. You want us to go talk to the hack? Let him know we'll consider it a personal insult if he doesn't check his frigging facts?"

His ardent defense brought a smile to her lips despite the onions. She could see it now—Local Politician's Career Goes Up in Flames Over Alleged Mob Association. Renzo and Nico—a former hockey star whose nose had been broken enough times to give new meaning to the phrase "angular features"—definitely looked the part.

Giselle nudged Renzo with a not-so-delicate elbow to the ribs. "Give her some room, will you? She's had a hell of a day." Turning to Summer her expression softened. "It's no crime to call for back-up. And even though Renzo likes to talk as if he's straight off the boat from Sicily, he can actually be fairly persuasive with nonviolent means."

"No." Much as Summer relished this new sense of family developing among her co-workers, she didn't have any intention of letting a man sail into her life to save her bacon. Not Renzo Cesare. And not Jackson Taggart. Assuming, of course, Jackson cared about her bacon one way or another. "Thanks, Renzo, but I'm going to ride this one out on my own. I've got a long history of running from my problems and I don't think it's really going to conquer that tendency if I simply hand off the problem to someone else, you know?''

Renzo shook his head before he stalked back to the brick ovens. "When did women get so damn independent? No offense, Summer, but you're as bad as my sister. One day you ladies will realize that there is a necessary cosmic order to the whole sex thing.''

Giselle whipped him in the back with a dishtowel. "Oh, right. You kick ass while we cook dinner. Check my bread, He-Man. You can save us from evil another day.''

The peal of a telephone ringer cut the sibling squabble short. Giselle and her brother both stared at Summer's chirping purse expectantly.

"I don't feel like talking to him yet." Summer moved the purse from a spare chair to under the counter. "I'm not ready to—"

A masculine voice spoke over top of her words. "Not ready to talk to anybody right after your first brush with negative press?" Jackson stood in the middle of the kitchen wearing a blue golf shirt and pressed khakis. Even dressed down he looked perfect. "Sucks when they hit below the belt like that, doesn't it?''

It did suck, as a matter of fact. Her throat suddenly scratched with the residual sting of the article now that Jackson was here and empathizing. Damn it, she hadn't felt a thing five minutes ago, and with one concerned look from Jackson she felt the full impact of having her past hung out to dry for public viewing. Had he interrupted his packed schedule just to be here for her today?

"No." She shook her head, denying it anyway.

"It's just the onions." Her voice broke on the last word and she caught a glimpse of Jackson heading toward her as a small sob slipped free.

By the time he was there, holding her while she cried for no good reason, Summer realized Giselle had hustled Renzo out of the room. Garlic bread now filled the pastry cart, its rich scent swirling around the kitchen and swamping her with the realization she hadn't eaten all day.

Or maybe she was hungry for a different kind of sustenance entirely, the kind only sexy lawyers in golf shirts could provide.

Closing her eyes, she allowed herself to lean into Jackson's strong arms, her head cradled in the nook between his neck and shoulder. Renzo Cesare might have had a point about a cosmic balance between the sexes, because leaning on Jackson right now felt very, very good.

"I'm so sorry about this," he whispered into her hair, his jaw flexing against her scalp, his hands rubbing up and down her back. Now and then his fingers grazed a patch of skin bared by her overalls, making her long for more skin-on-skin contact. "None of this would have happened if you hadn't been spotted with me."

"None of this would have happened if I hadn't been raised by such restless spirits who didn't know where to search for meaning in their lives, either, but that doesn't mean I regret the way I was brought up." She pulled away just enough to look up at him, to be sure he knew she meant what she said. "Just like I don't regret being with you."

"But our connection will continue to cause you

grief.'' His hand cupped her chin, his fingers stroked down along her jaw, the gentle touch sparking flames of awareness. ''I've been putting off my appointments today until we spoke because I need to know how you want me to respond to all this. I didn't want to just toss 'no comment' out there for hours on end when maybe I could nip this in the bud somehow for you.''

For her? Or for him? She hated that it mattered to her so much. If all they had between them was a simple relationship based on mutual gratification, then she shouldn't care whose butt he wanted to cover.

''Well, I can't will away my past as though it never happened.'' She stepped back, mourning the loss of his touch but hoping the additional breathing room would give her much-needed perspective. Distance.

She had to remember that while the article had emotional implications for her, for Jackson it had been a purely professional issue.

''I don't mean to suggest you should try to cover it up. I just want you to be aware the media will revisit this kind of thing again and again unless we can satisfy their curiosity enough to make them go away.'' He hesitated. ''Or unless you want to—''

The pop of a flashbulb cut him off, the burst of light making her see stars.

They turned toward the intrusion, found a twenty-something brunette in jeans and a slouchy T-shirt with a camera in hand. She waved a media badge clipped to her camera bag but Summer couldn't read it for the white spots still drifting through her field of vision.

Summer wanted to tell her where to get off, but the flash-happy brunette was too quick for her. ''Mr. Taggart, how did it make you feel to learn your girlfriend has ties to various underground cults with political agendas that run counter to your own? Should South Beach voters take this as a sign that you've changed your position on key issues in this election?''

Summer blinked while the brunette produced a tiny microphone.

Nausea rolled through her as she realized for the first time how much she had complicated Jackson's life. His career. After all the heat he'd taken in the wake of his father's scandal, he *so* didn't deserve this now.

He turned his head away from the microphone and leaned close to Summer. His voice whispered huskily across her ear. ''Meet me in the bordello in five. If you see cameras on the way, try to lose them. We don't need a media frenzy outside the door.''

They were going to be locked inside the bordello together in five minutes?

She made the mistake of meeting Jackson's gaze for a shocked moment. His blue eyes communicated a mutual longing for the privacy of that sensual haven.

The man's wild streak was growing by the hour if he would willingly retreat on a day when he surely needed to go on the offensive.

Still, with her temperature suddenly soaring into the red zone, she didn't have the option of playing the altruist right now. She wanted that time behind closed doors more than he could imagine.

Winking at him, Summer nudged by the photographer. ''Excuse me. I need to attend to some hotel business.''

Some bordello business, more precisely. Some

kinky, sexy, lock-up-that-man-of-mine business to put an even finer point on it.

As she sauntered through the hotel, cloak-and-dagger style, she remembered that first night when Jackson had followed her. Her intuition had made her hyperaware that night, too. Only then, she must have sensed the attraction even before she'd laid eyes on the man, because the feeling had been different, more intense.

Now, only a crusty reporter followed her, a man she'd ID'd by his notebook and his camera, and although her intuition told her she was being followed, there was none of the electric excitement she'd felt that first night.

Unless a girl counted the pulse of energy she experienced at the thought of Jackson joining her in the bordello. She had no idea how he could justify stealing away from the campaign trail for a few hours, but his eyes had communicated the desire as clearly as if he'd said as much.

Now she rode up the elevator and down the elevator for good measure, determined to lose her pursuer so she could take full advantage of whatever time Jackson had to offer today. In the wake of the crappy article on her past, her friends' support had buffered the blow and Renzo Cesare's offer to play hit guy had made her laugh, but only Jackson had the power to make her overlook the sting to her heart.

The promise of time alone with him, the lure of his simple touch promised total, delirious forgetting. And she craved that forgetting more than she wanted a printed retraction or a note of apology, or even a sudden case of broken legs for the reporter in question.

As she reached the stretch of corridor outside the bordello, she only hoped Jackson wanted that half as much as she did.

# 13

*Climbing into bed with your prey.*

JACKSON HAD speeches to give, hands to shake and voters to sway, yet here he was in the middle of a weekday at the start of his campaign doing something else entirely.

He haunted the corridors of Club Paradise like a lust-ridden ghost, intent only on stealing a few minutes with Summer. No doubt about it, he had lost sight of all his intelligent strategies to act on impulse, called to Summer's side just in case she needed him. Just in case the article had hurt her. That damn article had taught him he was only hurting her with his association, and he knew too soon he'd have to let her go. For her sake.

Hearing another hotel-room door open down the hall, he ducked into the nook where the pay phones and vending machines resided. Even though he realized he was ten times the fool for ignoring his well-planned itinerary to comfort Summer today, he had no intention of turning back on the errand now.

Comfort had turned heated until he had no choice but to seek privacy with her. Claim her as his if only for a few hours. His clandestine pursuit of her through the hotel rekindled vivid memories of their first meeting.

As he watched a graying reporter complete with straw hat and notebook hurry past his hiding place, Jackson thought back to that first night.

Too frustrated by the family scandal and embittered by his father's betrayal, Jackson hadn't even been sure he would commit himself to the political arena again. Somehow, time spent with Summer and her uninhibited, honest ways had renewed a glint of optimism he'd long thought dead. Her enthusiasm about sailing, a pastime his privileged family often took for granted, had made their day on the water a new experience for him. And hell, something about a woman in glitter seashell sunglasses would stir a smile to any guy's face.

He was going to miss that about her. Her total, kick-ass ability to make him smile, to take him by surprise.

But he wasn't letting go without one more chance to kiss her, touch her. Pretend she belonged to him.

Sensing the hall had cleared, Jackson edged closer to the bordello door, more sure he was doing the right thing by taking a time-out to be with her today. If not for Summer, he might not have found the passion to tackle an election so soon after the investigation of his father. She'd inspired him then and she supported him now more than his damn campaign manager.

To his way of thinking, a meeting with Summer in the bordello counted as necessary motivation time. His personal pep talk.

Oh yeah.

He'd barely grazed his knuckles across the door when it opened to admit him. Blues music floated on the air as he stepped inside. He didn't see her at first. The room was veiled in darkness although his wrist-watch registered midafternoon.

But he sensed her. Whether by the faint strawberry fragrance she favored or by some mysterious chemical lure of their undeniable attraction, he couldn't be sure. Summer would probably say he had ESP. Any way he looked at it, he simply *knew* she was off to his right, hedging in the shadows at the edge of his adjusting vision.

"I took the liberty of giving us a little privacy." Her voice drifted through the darkness from the direction he'd guessed.

Slowly, his eyes distinguished the outline of her leaning back against one velvet-covered wall. The pale contrast of her long, smooth legs with the dark wall drew his attention. Soon, he noticed she wasn't wearing her cut-off overalls and body-skimming T-shirt anymore, either. She'd found enough time while she waited for him, not only to darken the room, but she'd also slid into the rose-colored corset thing she had worn the night they met.

And—holy sexual healing—the outfit included rosy colored panties edged in naughty black lace.

"Privacy is good," he managed to croak past the lust lodged in his throat. His fingers itched to touch her. To claim her.

"Of course, I wouldn't want to take up too much of your time." She glanced at him through long, sly lashes.

She was so damn pretty, so full of life and willing to share herself with him.

"I want nothing more than to have you all to myself.'' And not just for today, damn it. He wanted her tomorrow, and the day after and the day after that. If only he could be impulsive enough to let their relationship ride…but he was too much of a strategist, too much of a planner for that kind of approach. And he couldn't stand to see their liaison raked over the coals until part of Summer's optimism died.

He wouldn't have her penchant for glitter sunglasses squelched because of his highly public lifestyle.

She hissed in a breath between her teeth, the soft sound drawing him near. ''Do you mind if we keep it dark in here? And if anybody knocks we'll pretend no one is home?''

Beginning to understand her thinking, he stalked closer, the need for her infusing his limbs, crawling over every inch of his skin. ''You think we can fool any reporters hanging around outside the door?'' Bracing his hands on the wall at either side of her, he caught her in a close trap, unwilling to let her go. He brought his lips mere inches from her ear. ''Because we can keep it dark, but I don't know that we can keep it quiet.''

A shiver trembled through her, her body slowly catching fire. ''Maybe if we take it easy we can be quiet?''

*Not a chance in hell.* He leaned in close enough to brush her cheek with his lips, her silky skin a temptation he couldn't resist. ''Do you want to take it easy today? Do you really want me to temper my touches so you don't cry out so loudly?''

Her head tipped back against the velvet-covered wall. ''Bad idea.'' Lifting one of the satin ribbons between her breasts, she smoothed the length between two fingers. "I think you know that's not what I want at all."

"You're right. What if I told you I know exactly what you want?" Images of her fantasy played through his mind. A need to be overpowered. He'd regret it forever if he didn't bring that fantasy to life. For him, for her...he didn't even know anymore. He simply saw the desire in her eyes, heard her body speak to his on the most primal level and made up his mind to indulge them both.

She shook her head, her blond hair dusting across bare shoulders. "You couldn't possibly know what a naughty girl I am on the inside, Jackson Taggart."

Reaching for the satin ribbon she still twisted with restless fingers, he brushed her hand aside to take charge of the delicate bow holding her outfit together.

"Or maybe *you* don't realize what depths of wickedness I would navigate to discover those dark fantasies of yours." Untying the bow at her breasts with deceptive gentleness, he allowed the garment to loosen just a fraction. Then he looped a finger through the twined ribbon at the hem of her garment and yanked the rest free.

Summer gasped as the silky corset slipped to the floor. A delicate shiver trembled over her, a tremor he could feel across the fraction of an inch that separated them.

His gaze dropped to the creamy fullness of her breasts, topped with pink, pebbled nipples that seemed to beg for his touch, his kiss.

She shifted on her bare feet, her thighs grazing his. "How could you know..."

As her words trailed off, he forced his eyes to meet hers. And he could see she remembered. She *knew*.

"You heard me confiding my fantasy to Brianne that night, didn't you?" The words carried a vague hint of accusation. A heavier dose of throaty arousal.

"I've been playing it out in my mind every second of every day since then." Smoothing his hands down the length of her arms he found her wrists and circled them with his fingers, lifted them over her head and held them together with one hand. Her breasts rose with the motion, promptly making his mouth water.

"Then you are definitely much more of a bad boy than I'd realized."

Bending to brush the soft weight of her curves with his lips, he nipped and licked a path between her breasts. "Now that you've learned the truth about me, you have a decision to make."

"Then you must not have heard my fantasy."

He released one rosy nipple long enough to meet her gaze.

She stirred against him, her body calling to his for attention. "Because if you had heard what I really crave the most, you would know I don't want it to involve me making a single decision."

Summer stared back at Jackson in the darkened room, and his blue eyes were alight with the fire leaping between them. Would he understand that she didn't want any political correctness infringing on her fantasy? She'd had to take charge of her life at a young age to escape her parents' unorthodox lifestyle. She'd taken on a staggering amount of responsibility at the resort when she'd promised her partners she'd redecorate the entire property on a shoestring budget. Right now, she wanted only to hand over all control to someone else, to put the power in Jackson's deliciously capable hands.

One sandy brow arched at her words, the only hint of surprise he betrayed. He let go of her wrists and ran his hands down to her waist, her hips. "Then loop your arms around my neck and hold on. Now." His voice didn't ask, it commanded.

She did as he told her, a whisper of excitement feathering over her as he lifted her in his arms and wrapped her legs around his hips.

He carried her to the bed but didn't release her. "Grab the comforter for me."

Arching back, she snagged a handful of red satin and tugged it off the bed, curious about what he had in mind.

Once she had retrieved it, he moved them to the middle of the room and shoved aside extra furnishings with his foot. "Lay it down."

She dropped the quilt on the floor and he lowered them to the silky blanket, smoothing and spreading the material wide around them. Summer reclined on her back, tickled by the cool sensation of satin along her shoulders and an incredibly hot male over top of her.

"You don't find the bed comfortable, counselor?" She smoothed her fingers down the placket of his golf shirt, unbuttoning as she went.

"I don't find the bed spacious enough for all the ways I want to take you." Levering up off her, he pulled his shirt over his head. His trousers, she noticed, remained in place as he settled on top of her.

"You won't be able to take much if you leave your

pants on.'' She reached for his belt buckle, eager to dispense with all the layers between them.

His hand gripped her wrist and tugged it to the side of her head, pinning her lightly to the floor. ''How quickly you forget who's in charge here. Why don't you just be still and see what happens?''

As he spoke, he tugged her other hand into position on the other side of her head, the back of her fingers sinking into the plump depths of quilted satin.

Warm honey seemed to flow through her veins, every inch of her sticky and sweet on the inside. She shrugged a shoulder as if it didn't matter that she had to wait to get what she wanted.

''Do your worst, Jack.''

''I fully intend to.'' He lowered more of his weight on her, allowing her to feel the thick heat of his lower body molded to hers.

She closed her eyes, relaxing into the sensation of relinquishing control. Instead of thinking about what would happen next, she simply breathed in Jackson, his scent, his warmth, his hunger. She remembered that he'd chased her here, to this very room that first night. He had listened to her tell Brianne about what she'd wanted from a man, which was probably just as well since she never would have confided such a thing to him. He'd pursued her with relentless persistence even when she said no.

And wow, had that ever turned her on.

The man had skillfully maneuvered her into one date, and then another. He'd forced her to look at him as a contender for a relationship and not just a one-night sensual treat.

His hands still held her wrists to keep her in place,

his breath a slow, even puff across her bare breasts as he lowered his head closer and closer to her exposed nipples.

Resisting the urge to open her eyes, Summer flexed her fingers to test his resolve when it came to pinning her down.

He didn't budge. Neither did her wrists.

Her heart picked up the pace, slugging harder and faster against the chest he seemed to be deliberating over. Her skin tingled, her nipples tightening to an almost painful degree. His mouth ought to be so close now...

And then he licked his way around one stiff peak.

Summer's back bowed, her shoulders all but lifting off their silken spread in order to increase the pressure of his mouth on her. He only backed up as she came forward, thwarting her efforts and keeping her just where he wanted her.

"Wicked man." She settled back into her satin prison.

"Greedy woman," he whispered back as he transferred his attention from one breast to the other. "You think you can be very, very still if I let go of you?"

"I think I might tackle you and have my way with you." Tension thrummed through her as the heat grew between her legs.

"But then you'll never know what you might have missed out on. Besides, if I have to hold you down, then you miss out on what I do with my hands." For emphasis, he traced delicate circles on the inside of her arm with his fingers.

She had enough imagination to envision that tight

circle drawn somewhere else on her body. Somewhere far more useful. "You can let go."

"Promise me you'll stay put."

When she hesitated, he adjusted the position of his thigh between hers, increasing the pressure to the place that needed him most, then withdrew. Summer nearly cried out at the loss of that touch, her eyes flying open.

"I promise."

"Stay right there." He let go of her wrists, slowly, almost as if he didn't trust her not to tackle him. "You've got an armoire full of slinky stockings I can use to tie you up if you don't cooperate."

"Just please..." The edgy hunger burned over her, desperate for his touch. "Please touch me."

She watched him peruse her almost naked body with frank male appreciation and the slow thoughtfulness of a man looking for a place to start.

Sliding lower on their makeshift bed, Jackson paused when his lips hovered above her navel. Although she mentally willed him a bit further south, he paused to kiss the soft skin of her belly and the curve of one hip.

Sensation rocked through her lower body, skipping from her limbs to concentrate between her thighs. A moan built in her throat, a needy cry for more, but his hands slipped beneath her to dance along the backs of her legs before she could utter a sound.

As he kissed his way down her body, he traced more circles with his fingers in all the wrong places. Behind one knee, inside her thigh, but not *there*, where she needed him.

Her hips twitched with impatience just as his mouth met the waistband of her panties, his tongue straying beneath the scrap of material. His breath fanned over her skin, leaving a momentary damp heat, a subtle steam that left her craving a deeper touch.

Patience was rewarded when he tugged the panties lower with his teeth, slowly dragging the silk down her thighs. She nearly came out of her skin when he hovered above the juncture of her thighs just long enough to whisper a breath across the heated center of her. With efficient hands, he whisked away the silk twisted around her knees and rose to lie beside her.

Summer couldn't suppress the cry in her throat this time.

"Shh." He whispered to her as he propped himself on an elbow, his long, lean body stretched out on the red satin. "I want to watch you come."

He spread her legs with one hand before slipping a finger deep inside her. And then another.

She moaned with this new level of satisfaction, her hips automatically grinding a rhythm against his palm. He watched her in rapt fascination, his avid blue gaze missing nothing. Unwilling to reveal too much to this man, she closed her eyes and concentrated on his touch, his scent, his heat.

Within seconds she was panting on the verge of the orgasm that had been tickling her insides ever since he'd pinned her to one velvet wall of the bordello. His hands moved in delicious time to the sexy blues tune drifting from the nightstand radio. He whispered words of praise, words of encouragement through the veil of her hair into her ear.

And finally, when she thought she could stand no more of his slow rhythm, he slid his fingers to the throbbing heart of her and traced that deliberate, tight circle around her.

Her thighs clenched and the delicate muscles inside her contracted again and again, squeezing the very core of her as she flew apart in a million directions. White lights spotted the backs of her eyelids in a dizzying streak as Jackson carried her through every last tremor.

She didn't think her breath would ever return to normal. Air huffed in and out of her lungs at breakneck speed. Only when Jackson shifted beside her did she remember there was more to come.

Or so she hoped.

"I want—" she started, but he sealed her lips with the soft pad of his thumb.

"Sweetheart, I just gave you plenty of what you wanted. Don't you think it's time we thought about what I might want from you?" He slid his belt off and shoved to his feet to remove the rest of his clothes.

Summer watched him as he stood over her, unwilling to retreat behind closed eyes again. He looked— huge. Hot. Hard.

All the things she needed right now.

"And just what do *you* want?" She reached her foot to caress his calf, desperate to be in contact with any part of him.

"I want to be inside you right now." He rolled a condom over an impressive erection while she watched, fascinated. "And you're damn well going to accommodate me."

"I can't wait." She skimmed her hands across her breasts and down her belly to her thighs. She'd never been so bold before, but something about Jackson's conservative side assured her she could push the boundaries of his wild side and still be safe. Secure. And challenged. "I'm going to squeeze you so tight you're going to lose your mind. And I'm going to watch while every fantastic inch of you disappears in me."

A smile hitched at his lips before he turned to pluck two pillows off the bed.

"There might be a problem with that plan, gorgeous." He tossed the pillows on the floor beside her then knelt down on the satin.

"A problem?" Distracted by flexing muscles and a straining cock, Summer couldn't help but stare at him. The word *magnificent* continually ran through her mind as she absorbed every solid plane of his male body.

"A definite problem." He leaned over her to slide a hand around her back. His erection nudged her thigh and sent another wave of heat rolling through her. "You're not going to be able to watch when you're on your hands and knees."

# *14*

_____

*When backed into a corner, even the most skilled hunt-*
*ers retaliate with a roar of their own.*

JACKSON WAITED, holding his breath and hoping he
hadn't overplayed his hand. He wanted her so badly
he would take her any way he could have her right
now, but somehow it seemed important to complete
the fantasy with the most obvious male-dominant sex
position.

Not that adopting the role was exactly a hardship.
Ever since he'd heard Summer confide her forbidden
longings to her girlfriend, he'd dreamed of this scenario many times.

Summer blinked up at him, her long platinum hair
partially shielding her pale body, and her wide gray
eyes making her look vulnerable. He half-considered
calling the words back when he noticed the quick,
shallow breaths she took. The deliberate way she bit
her lip.

"Oh yeah? *Make me.*"

He hoped like hell that was an invitation. It sure
sounded like an invitation, but he'd lost so much damn
blood to the massive erection he was sporting that he
wasn't entirely sure he had enough available to properly operate his brain.

His decision made for him when he saw the wicked gleam in her eyes, Jackson flipped her to her belly and onto the pillows before he drove himself insane with wondering.

Jamming the satin-covered feather pillow beneath her body to support her, he leaned back on his haunches to admire his handiwork—and nearly lost it staring at the picture she made.

The slope of her back curved invitingly, her hair trailing down to the middle of her spine. Her waist dipped in before her hips flared back out to the lush, pale bottom.

Control no longer an option, he positioned himself behind her and slid a hand around her waist, tugging her to him. He edged her thighs apart as far as he could before nudging his way inside, inch by mind-blowing inch.

He cupped her breasts in one hand, plumping them together to better tease the nipples with his thumb. Her throaty sighs encouraged him, drew his fingers to twine in the short curls between her legs and then play in the slick folds that surrounded him.

Her breathing grew ragged along with his until he felt his release coming up on him too damn hard, too fast. He plucked at the delicate center of her just in time, drawing another orgasm from deep within her moments before he came inside her.

Sensation ripped through him so hard he thought he'd black out on her.

A hell of a note to end on.

Instead, he managed to fall into the tangled mass of satin and pillows with her. Their bodies still locked, they lay spooned together as their breathing slowed, heartbeats eased.

The sweet strains of Ella Fitzgerald floated over them in their dark, seductive haven. Bodies cooling as reason returned, Jackson didn't have a clue where to go from here.

He'd just lived her fantasy that had become his. And by the very nature of their intimacy he felt a primal connection to her. More than that, he couldn't help but think he'd claimed her somehow.

And damned if that didn't feel good.

He wasn't sure how long they lay there in the dark. Long enough for the reality of their situation to hammer home all over again. Long enough for him to remember why he'd sought her out today.

The article. The negative publicity her resort would receive.

Logically, he knew it made the most sense for them to walk away from this attraction. Summer had said herself she couldn't be counted on to stick around South Beach forever. His career demanded a stability that would drive her crazy. Stifle her adventurous spirit. And one day, lead her to resent him.

But the idea of walking away bothered him on a fundamental level. He'd never been the kind of person to start something he couldn't finish. More than that, Summer had come to mean something to him... probably more than he cared to analyze... already.

Before he could figure out where to go next, her voice wafted across the red satin as she turned to face him. "If you were me, what would you do in response to the newspaper article?"

Surprised she would ask for his opinion, he weighed his thoughts, not wanting to blow his first chance at input.

"Hard to say when I don't know how you feel about your past or how close you are to your folks." He hammered the pillow that had wound up beneath his head in an effort to get comfortable. Damned near impossible considering he felt uncomfortable from the inside out with this discussion. "I can tell you what I told the papers after the scandal broke about my father burying evidence to protect his own investments when he worked as an FBI director. I made it clear I supported my father, but I didn't support his actions. And no matter how many questions they asked me about the situation, I just repeated the comment like a mantra. Eventually they left me alone and turned the focus back to my dad instead of me."

She reached behind her to tug a corner of red satin over her shoulder, bundling her inside a lush, touch-me exterior even though Jackson knew damn well how vulnerable she was beneath. "I don't know that I have enough resolve to keep my comments simple. I've never been the kind of person to censor my actions or my words."

"You shouldn't have to censor yourself." He hated to think about her weighing her words for his sake. Refusing to read palms or make total strangers smile with her astrological predictions. "It's not fair of me to ask you to subject yourself to all the public scrutiny that I go through on a daily basis. Part of the reason I'm drawn to you is your unconventional approach, yet that spark of difference is what will continually bring the media sniffing around your door and asking questions.''

The song on the radio shifted to a Billie Holiday ballad filled with heartache. The lady singing the blues seemed to echo the mood in the bordello. Or at least, his mood. He feared where this conversation headed…a one-way ticket to the end of a very good thing.

But he couldn't work a relationship this way, had never been a one-day-at-a-time kind of guy. He understood why being with him was difficult for her. Did she have any idea how difficult it had been for *him* to cross his fingers and hope she'd make a few concessions?

Summer's gray eyes searched his. ''Maybe if we lay low until after the election. And then…who knows? Maybe we could sneak in a few dates once you're settled in your new job.''

Jackson knew how much that bit of forward planning had cost the woman who never looked beyond today. His chest squeezed with a painful twinge. Guilt, regret…he couldn't be sure.

''But what about the election after that? And hell, even if I decided not to follow the family legacy of politics, just the Taggart name still attracts the spotlight. My cousins end up in the paper along with my aunts, my uncles and my mother's domestic help. We're a bona fide southern Florida three-ring circus.'' A never-ending source of interest for the media, along with anyone attached to them.

She studied him thoughtfully. He could practically see the wheels turning in her mind. Finally, she took a deep breath. ''I'm not worried.''

"Damn it, Summer, you ought to be." How could she even think about getting involved with the mess that his life had become? He could date a kindergarten teacher and the press would manage to unearth something scandalous to put in the paper on the poor woman. And Summer Farnsworth was no kindergarten teacher. "Club Paradise is your livelihood. You can't afford to have negative press attached to your business."

"I told you before, publicity of any kind packs the house at the Moulin Rouge Lounge every night. We'll probably have record crowds tonight." She tilted her chin, showing off a stubborn side he hadn't seen before.

And she was being stubborn about fighting for their relationship. God, he was a heel for trying to discourage her now after all he'd done to entice her in the first place.

"The nightclub might benefit, but that's only a fraction of your business. Over the long haul, the resort will suffer from this kind of exposure."

Summer sidled out of her red satin cocoon and rose to her feet, looking for all the world like Lady Godiva with her long blond hair covering the most delicious aspects of her nakedness.

Good thing for that silky platinum veil or he might have forgotten what was really important here. Saving Summer from their recklessness.

Or—much more appealing—tying her to him for the long haul so they could figure things out *together*.

"I don't know what makes you think I would be the kind of person who would crumble in the face of one little article, Jackson." She stormed her way across the room to the armoire and dragged out the T-shirt and overalls she'd been wearing earlier. With sharp, pointed movements, she stepped into the garments and yanked them into place. "I know I told you that I don't tend to stay in one place for too long, but that doesn't mean I run at the first sign of adversity. I might walk away when I get bored, but I've sure as hell never backed down from a fight."

Considering the fierce look in her eye, he damn well believed her. He scrambled to his feet, sensing the need to explain himself.

She held up a hand as if to ward off explanations. "But don't worry, I'm getting the sense that this discussion isn't about how I handle the media so much as it's about me and you."

He pulled on his pants, following her as she moved toward the mirror and began smoothing her tousled hair. "I wish it didn't have to be about me and you. And I damn well would rather be together aside from all the controversy, but this obviously isn't going to play out according to my personal wish list."

She whirled away from the mirror to face him, her wild mane of bed-rumpled hair remaining untamed. "Therefore you give up?"

The gentle fragrance of strawberries drifted to his nose along with the sweet scent of her skin that was uniquely hers. He wanted nothing more than to crawl back into bed with her and take up where they'd left off, but that didn't solve the real-world problems this relationship created for them both.

He reached for her, his hands smoothing down the length of her bare arms. "No. Therefore I can see what's best for you and know I'm only being selfish by asking you to go out with me, be seen with me, to do the whole dating thing. I know you didn't want that from the beginning, but I hounded you because I wanted more than some temporary fling. Now I can see where my demands were unfair and out of line.''

His thumbs smoothed over her shoulder, past the brassy overall hooks that held her outfit together to trace the delicate slope of her collarbone. She was such a mix of vulnerability and bad-girl attitude. He didn't think he would ever get tired of exploring her wealth of contradictions. ''But damn it, Summer, I can't pretend that I don't want more from you. I've never been the kind of guy to hang out with a wait-and-see attitude, and I don't know how long I can wait for you to decide to make some kind of commitment here.''

Summer blinked, struggling to keep up with this conversation she *sooo* didn't want to have right now. She'd just experienced the best sex of her life, and perhaps due to the very aggressive nature of their interaction, she also happened to feel far more vulnerable than she ever had after a roll in the hay.

This time had been different. Special. Scary on a deep, emotional level.

''So what do you say, Summer?'' He sifted his fingers through her hair before tilting her chin to meet his gaze. By now, her eyes had grown accustomed to the dark enough to see the intensity of his stare. ''Do you trust in us? In me? Can we take this relationship to the next level?''

He wanted more?

She swallowed. Scared. Edgy. Fighting the urge to flee. She turned away, not ready to go head to head with a trial lawyer when it came time for a serious discussion. Sliding into a pair of old purple tennis shoes she tried not to look at Jackson, his bare chest enough to make her want to go running back to his arms and forget that he wanted more from her.

"I thought today demonstrated a healthy dose of trust." She gestured vaguely toward the satin comforter where he'd so totally rocked her world. Didn't he see how much trust it had taken to completely give up the reins to him?

She'd never been one to spell out her emotions for anyone. For that matter, she'd never stuck around long enough to get her emotions involved before, so this was all new, terrifying terrain for her.

He stalked closer, pursuing her around the room the same way he had that very first night. Only now, he wasn't pushing for just a date. Now, Summer knew, he would push for more than she was ready to give.

Or walk away without looking back.

"You're right." Jackson's hands seized her hips, his fingers straying over the curve of her bottom and reminding her of the way they'd experienced total sensual meltdown together. "Today you showed me a kind of physical trust you've never given to me before. But now that our relationship has been cast into the pressure cooker, I need to know if you're going to be able to go forward with me. I'm not the kind of guy to keep things superficial, Summer. I'm thinking more along the lines of…long-term."

Fear bubbled in time with his words. She'd never done anything long-term.

Still, something stirred deep inside her at his words. A forgotten optimism that she'd banished from her life after losing too many friends to the relentless pace of moving from town to town and cult to cult. For the first time, she really wished she could trust in something for more than a few months.

But the risks…

The potential for devastating hurt loomed. And now that she was seriously toying with the idea of staying in South Beach on a permanent basis, the consequences for failure with Jackson were all the higher. She wouldn't be able to simply pick up and run.

Hurt and panic chasing one another until her gut swirled with worry, Summer had no choice but to tell him exactly how she felt. "I can't help it that your career has put us on some kind of hyper-speed countdown to commitment. I'm not ready to make the kind of leap that you want, and, frankly, I don't know that I ever will be."

Not giving herself a chance to change her mind, she reached blindly for the door and made her exit. And unlike that first night when he pursued her around the bordello suite, this time, he let her.

"No COMMENT."

Jackson repeated the same phrase he'd been doling out to reporters all week in his latest phone interview with a local radio station. Thanks to the wonders of modern technology, he could at least conduct this piece of business via cell phone from the relative comfort of a lounge chair parked on the beach—situated roughly a hundred yards from where the Moulin Rouge Lounge now celebrated toga-party happy hour on the multilevel deck overlooking the ocean.

Hell, if he was forced to listen to questions about

Summer in every damn interview he conducted, he figured he might as well at least have the pleasure of looking at her while he spoke.

He scanned the early-evening crowd for a glimpse of her as the DJ interviewing him rephrased his question about Summer another way.

"Sorry, Stu," Jackson struggled to smile as he said the words so his voice would reflect a light note he didn't feel, "but I can't comment about that. If you want to talk zoning laws to protect our beaches from overdevelopment, however, I'm ready when you are."

Crisis averted, Jackson went on to discuss how local zoning laws could have a bigger impact on the environment, a topic he and Summer had discussed at length that day on his boat. He wondered if she ever listened to his interviews and campaign speeches or if she had completely tuned him out.

Damn but this week without her had been killing him. Especially when all his new campaign literature boasted her design work. Everywhere he looked, he saw reminders of her generosity, her energetic spirit.

He wrapped things up on the phone just as he caught a glimpse of wispy platinum-blond hair falling over a—Christ—*silver* toga. Even from a hundred yards away he knew he'd spotted Summer.

He would have been content to track her movements around the deck, but his campaign manager returned to Jackson's side, arms loaded down with confiscated glasses of ice tea and bowls of tortilla chips.

Lucky dropped into the lounger beside him, settling their scant attempt at dinner on the leather briefcase that never left Lucky's side. "They were all out of extrahot, my friend." He plunked down a ceramic container of salsa. "You're going to have to settle for medium."

Jackson had to force himself to tear his eyes away from the silver toga and concentrate on work. His campaign would fall apart if he didn't get his mind on the election race instead of the constant ache in his chest since Summer had walked away.

"Screw medium. I'd rather choke them down plain." Jackson knew he sounded like a goddamn diva and didn't have a clue how to make himself shut up. When a man wanted something spicy, no amount of mild, milk-toast substitute would cut it.

And hell yeah, after you had a shot at the woman in the silver toga, you couldn't go back to lady lawyers who favored conservative suits.

Or even bikini-clad twins like the identical blond sun worshippers scoping out him and Lucky on the beach right now.

Jackson shook his head as the women waggled come-hither fingers in their direction.

They giggled, their fair heads tilted together as they plotted something. One of them cupped her hands around her mouth and shouted over, "If you're busy, how about we both take him?"

Good God, they were pointing at Lucky.

His campaign manager—some kind of freaking chick magnet or something?—smiled, thanked the twins and waved them off with a vague "maybe later."

Jackson shook his head, having no clue what women saw in his slick-talking, power-broker manager. Maybe some women found that fierce determination attractive, but damn. Jackson might be driven, but Lucky Adams single-mindedly pursued the fast track to bigger and better.

Jackson sighed and munched his chips with the crappy salsa wishing he could be a chick magnet with one woman only.

"If you're turning down twins, I'm going to go out on a limb and say you're still missing the hot-tamale girlfriend." Lucky chugged his ice tea and loosened his tie in deference to the beach weather.

"Not that it's any of your business, but maybe I am." He hadn't been expecting her to turn the tables on him the way she had. He'd treated their conversation like a damn cross-examination that day, pushing her to get what he wanted instead of letting her set her own pace.

No wonder she'd balked.

Lucky shoved off his shoes and leaned back in the lounger, obviously soaking up the Friday happy-hour mentality of the partying crowd a few palm trees down the shore. "I thought it would make our job easier to have her out of the picture, but now that she's gone, I'm wondering if maybe you made a mistake."

"A mistake?" Jackson gulped down a swig of tea to cool the angry fire slowly coming to life inside him. Did Lucky think to interfere with his personal life again?

"I'm just wondering if your girlfriend might have been an asset after all. Sure, her unorthodox clothes and her unconventional past can be detriments to your image, but those are the same things that appeal to the younger set. South Beach actually has a very high number of twenty-something voters." He moved the chips off his briefcase to reach inside the leather pouch. "I think I have the demographic breakdown in here somewhere. Maybe we can figure out mathematically if her usefulness outweighs the potential harm she can do."

Jackson would have slugged his jerk-off campaign manager if he hadn't realized that Summer would have howled with laughter at the guy. No doubt she'd get a kick out of having her assets mathematically computed.

"I don't think that's necessary." Jackson contented himself with slamming Lucky's overstuffed piece of luggage back into the sand. "In fact, trying to put a numerical value on Summer's worth would really piss me off right now."

"Moot point since I can't find those demographics anyway," Lucky continued, unruffled. "But my whole point was going to be that she might have been contributing more to your campaign then you realized."

Shoving aside his personal annoyance with the guy, Jackson tried to figure out what he meant. Lucky Adams might be a thorn in his side, but he sure as hell knew his job or Jackson never would have hired him.

"I don't know about that. It's not like she went out campaigning with me." Jackson had been thinking he could make the campaign work with or without her.

Though he hadn't realized getting through the election would be sort of like stabbing himself with a sharp stick without her by his side.

Lucky glanced back to the deck where the party milled. "Still, maybe you were a better candidate when she was part of your life, you know? Not to knock your speeches this week or anything, but you seemed to have a lot more enthusiasm for the whole thing before she dumped you."

"She didn't dump me." Not in so many words anyway. She just didn't want to commit. And damn it, he was tired of chasing her around to pin her down for more. "For your information, I'm goddamn enthused about the campaign, with Summer or without her. Now, can we move away from hypothesizing here and get back to business?" He dug into the chip bowl for a handful of tortillas and even dunked them into the tasteless salsa. No way would he go down that road of should-haves with his bottom-line-oriented manager.

He'd trod that terrain enough on his own, thank you very much.

"Fine by me. I'm sure you'll drum up the necessary fervor for your speech at the South Beach historical society tomorrow. They're expecting capacity crowds to hear you talk about beach preservation." Lucky wiped the excess chip crumbs from his suit. "And I only brought up your ex-girlfriend because I hear she's giving a big press conference of her own tomorrow."

The tortillas stuck in his throat. "Summer?"

"That's the buzz among the happy-hour crowd." Lucky juggled a cell phone while he circled numbers in the financial section and tossed chips in his mouth.

Jackson sat up in his lounger, his gaze hunting for a glimpse of silver again. Did she plan to confront the media about the article on her past? "That's all you heard?"

Screw trying to pretend he didn't care. He needed details.

"I guess she's got *Wanderlust* magazine coming out here to do a feature spread on the rooms she decorated at the resort. If the piece runs, it will be great exposure.

Not just for Club Paradise, but for all of South Beach.''

It could be a career-making moment for her.

A favorable pictorial in *Wanderlust* would be an endorsement worth big bucks to the hotel. But would it be enough to tie Summer to South Beach?

Jackson finally spotted her gliding among the rowdy patrons on the back deck, a radiant column of platinum-topped silver among a sea of shapeless white togas. He wanted her so much his eyes damn near crossed.

Lucky followed his gaze and grinned. ''What do you think, Jack? You going to try to win her back?''

Hell, yeah.

''Between you and me, I probably made a big mistake letting her walk away. And not because she has some bullshit favorable value to my campaign.'' He should have never tried to rush her into a commitment she wasn't ready to give. Hadn't he learned his lesson about finding balance in life?

''You're crazy about her, aren't you?''

As if he'd bare his heart to his joker campaign manager who'd just last week tried to tell him Summer's notoriety would infringe on the election race.

He'd give Summer some space to conduct her big press conference with *Wanderlust* magazine and then he was going to beg her to let him be a part of her life on her own time frame...no pressure. He'd be damn fortunate if she gave him the time after all his pushy tactics.

He was through mixing up the boundaries between his personal and professional life.

''For the record, Lucky, I've got no comment.''

# 15

_Be careful about lowering your defenses._

"THE PAPER says your ex-boyfriend is 'no-commenting' himself right into a sliding popularity rating with voters," Giselle called up to Summer from her perch in the bordello suite's gold wingback chair. "What do you think of that, Ms. Power-Behind-the-Throne?"

Summer stood carefully balanced on the arm of the chair, praying she wouldn't inadvertently land in Giselle's lap while she tried to straighten a piece of shirred velvet material on one wall of the soon-to-be photographed room.

"I think that editorial grossly overstates my influence on the man's popularity." Summer hammered a tiny nail into the errant piece of fabric, careful not to chip the manicure she'd spent an hour on last night.

As if she hadn't heard a word of Summer's reply, Giselle forged ahead as she scanned the morning edition of the weekly South Beach tabloid. "The writer calls you Jackson's muse and suggests that, 'like Sampson without his hair, Jackson Taggart's strength throughout South Beach is diminished without the region's favorite daughter by his side.'"

Thwack.

"Ow!" Summer slammed her forefinger with the hammer. Somehow, she'd landed squarely on the pad of the digit as opposed to her nail. Hallelujah. She'd be black and blue for a week but by God, her manicure remained flawless. "Do you mind if we delete Jackson from all discussion today until after the *Wanderlust* crew leaves? I'm so nervous I can't see straight, let alone think about a man who has no time for developing a relationship and whose number-one concern is the bottom line."

She leaped to the floor, finger throbbing and long, semiconservative skirt flying. Of course, the pain in her hand didn't come close to the aching heart she'd been nursing all week, but damn it, she couldn't afford distractions of any kind today.

And Jackson Taggart counted as one big, gorgeous distraction in her book.

Damn the man and his pushy agendas. She actively sought out her anger at him, always a little more steady on her feet when she could embrace the fury instead of acknowledging the hurt his absence from her life had caused.

"Whoops." Giselle jammed the newspaper underneath the chair cushion and nodded contritely. "Not a problem."

Summer reached beneath the cushion and pulled the paper back out again. "It's not that much of a whoops. I can handle talking about him normally…" Her gaze landed on the newspaper photos. One of a stern-faced Jackson addressing students at the University of Miami this week. Another of him kissing the living daylights out of Summer on his boat. Her heart clenched, profoundly empty. "I just can't talk about him today when I need to get so much done."

Giselle stood, sliding the paper from Summer's fingers. "Sorry. I'll just go stick this in the oven and set it to torch, then I'll be back to help you prep."

Summer sighed as she watched her friend depart. She couldn't believe Jackson had once told her she possessed the Midas touch.

Not today! Everything she came in contact with seemed to fall apart this morning while she waited for the camera crew that could change her life and bring huge success to Club Paradise. The section of velvet had peeled off the wall in the bordello suite, probably a delayed effect of her and Jackson playing sensual power games with her pressed up again the wall. Then the editorial about her and Jackson had appeared— right when she couldn't afford to think about it. Then she'd flattened her finger, and now she'd managed to chase off her one lifeline for support.

Well done.

She hid all evidence of her fast fix on the wall, tossing the hammer under the bed. According to her astrological calendar, the stars had earmarked the day as "challenging" anyhow. Of course, Summer couldn't reschedule the shoot on the basis of negative planetary alignment.

Even *she* was grounded enough to realize corporate America would write her off as a flake if she did that. Better to deal with the possible fallout then blow her chance at the publicity Club Paradise desperately needed.

Still, the star outlook didn't help her nerves, especially when the prediction had proved accurate so far.

Now, she needed to go over her suggested itinerary for the magazine's visit, personally walk through all the rooms to be sure everything looked up to speed, run through her answers to potential sticky questions one more time, find out where the hell the fresh flowers were that should be in all the rooms already...

All that before the crew from *Wanderlust* arrived in what...she glanced down at her watch and felt the heart attack kick in.

Ten minutes.

Sprinting through the corridors of Club Paradise in the most conservative gold sandals she owned, Summer willed her half-hearted attempt at an upswept hairdo to stay in place.

Although she'd been mentally thumbing her nose at Jackson and his hyper-organized strategic maneuvering, she had to admit that she probably wouldn't be sweating from every available pore right now if she had her act together in true Taggart fashion. Maybe if she lived her life continually in the public eye, dependent upon public good will the way Jackson had, she would be more apt to plan ahead. In fact, she'd gladly sell off her every last Tarot deck for a little strategic planning right now.

*And* someone else to do the interview with *Wanderlust.*

She was good at the artsy end of design, but she really hated this being her own pitch person stuff. In a flash of realization, she couldn't help a twinge of empathy for Jackson who not only had to come up with cool tax plans and intelligent zoning laws to benefit the environment as much as the tourist trade, but he had to sell them to the public, as well. Definitely not an easy job.

Especially when the rest of the world wanted to make politics so completely personal.

She picked up copies of the media itinerary from Brianne's high-tech security office. Before she could start the walk-through of the first place on her list, Lainie tracked her down in the hallway, her sleek blond hair bouncing just a little in time to her determined steps.

"I just got a call from the front desk," she called, her voice cool and unflappable despite her charge down the corridor. "A camera crew just arrived on site. They should be meeting you in the bordello suite any minute."

Perhaps Summer's sheer terror showed on her face because Lainie's voice softened. "What can I do?"

"Kill me now and get it over with?"

Lainie shook her head, gently tugging one of the itineraries from Summer's sweaty grip. "Not an option. Next idea?"

"I need someone to walk through all the rooms on the list and make sure everything is camera-perfect. I never thought they'd be on time today, let alone ten minutes early."

"Done. Brianne and I will split the task and make sure you're on target. Anything else?" Lainie blinked up at her, waiting for further commands as if *Summer* were the CEO in this picture.

Her heart swelled at the friendship she'd found here, the total acceptance of her cards and crystals, her odd fashion sense and her hodgepodge of assorted talents. She'd probably been subconsciously hunting for this kind of sisterhood her entire life. And her parents were still on the move, searching for a bigger sense of community to belong to. She had found something too special here ever to leave it behind. Not even a painful break-up would make her run this time.

No matter how much losing Jackson had hurt.

Acting on impulse, she flung her arms around Lainie's slender shoulders encased in a perfectly tailored suit. "No. You're too good to me already."

She released Lainie, only to find her friend wide-eyed and looking a bit shell-shocked. Summer briefly intuited major personal-space issues from Lainie's aura, but she would have to investigate that path another day. Right now, she needed to meet that camera crew before she let down this newfound, eclectic collection of family.

Landing an awkward pat on Summer's shoulder, Lainie strode away, list in hand. Summer didn't even bother to be dignified. She hauled ass down the Club Paradise corridor and skidded to a stop just outside the bordello suite—just as a troop of strangers rounded the corner, hefting cameras and video recorders, their shoulders weighted down by black bags full of God-knows-what they needed for their trade.

Summer smiled her best engaging politician grin. She didn't imagine she looked quite so winning as Jackson Taggart when he turned on the charm, but at least she had a good mental model to work from. The man put the sugar in sweet talk, and that was no lie.

But as the camera crew neared, Summer realized they weren't exactly strangers after all.

She spotted the crusty old guy with the notebook who had chased her and Jackson through the club just last week. Then she spied the flashbulb-popping brunette who had snapped their photo in the kitchen.

This was definitely not the *Wanderlust* crew.

"Wait a minute." She halted just outside the door to the bordello suite. "I don't think we have an appointment."

The brunette stepped forward and offered her hand. "Sheena McClellan from the South Beach paper. We got wind of your spread in *Wanderlust* and thought we'd come down to do a feature on it. Sort of a photo shoot about a photo shoot, you know? The success or failure of Club Paradise will have a resounding effect on the local merchants so I think there will be plenty of reader interest."

Great. Just great.

Summer had no idea if she had the legal right to send them all packing. Besides, maybe Lainie would be thrilled to have the additional exposure.

Praying for a cool head and the budget to hire a dedicated public relations professional down the road, Summer shook the woman's hand. "Thanks so much for coming. I have an itinerary of the shots I'm lining up for the magazine right here. Why don't you glance over them and feel free to take a self-guided tour while I prepare to greet my guests?"

Willing her nervous hands not to shake, she passed Sheena a copy of the schedule and hoped she sounded remotely smooth and calm. She would never play PR person again. Never ever. No wonder she hadn't been able to make things work with Jackson Taggart. He could tattoo every limb of his body and she still wouldn't be able to stand calmly at his side while the media looked her over like a chicken for the plucking.

She'd been able to handle being a target for press interest when it didn't matter what they might print about her. But when the pressure was on to inspire good copy in tomorrow's edition, Summer wanted to run screaming in the other direction.

Sheena of the massive camera bag glanced over the itinerary and nodded. "We'll do our best to stay in the background." With a jerk of her head, she jump-started the small throng milling behind her. "Thanks for having us."

As if she had hosted them willingly.

Holding her plastered-on smile in place until the whole troop marched past, Summer looked forward to escaping into the suite to get her head together for even thirty seconds before she went on to face the cameras.

A noise sounded in the hall as she clicked open the lock however. Panicked, she braced herself for more smiling and looked up to find Giselle hustling down the hallway with an oversize room-service cart weighed down with food, her mile-long hair gathered in a loose updo that bounced in time to her walk.

"Amen." This she could handle. Besides, she needed to see Giselle to apologize for being so damned touchy earlier. "Sorry about flying off the handle before—"

Giselle cruised to a stop and aligned her cart against one wall. "Male-induced behavior. Trust me, I recognize it well and I can hardly hold it against you. I put the blame firmly in their court when my girlfriends start losing their minds."

"Ohmigod, you think that's what's happening to me?" Summer snitched a salmon-smothered cracker from the trays stuffed full of mouth-watering hors d'oeuvres.

"Of course. I also happen to think you're falling madly in love, but I won't mention that moments before you go on camera before a national audience."

Summer reeled. The cracker in her mouth went dry.

"Whoops, did that slip out?" Giselle patted Summer's back to keep her from choking. "Honey, honestly, thinking of that man puts amazing color in your cheeks so I actually just did you a big favor. You can deny it all day and pretend you're too cool to stick around long enough to start a massive relationship, but the fact remains, you've got it bad."

In love with Jackson? Her heart did a ridiculous flip as she stood there holding the door to the suite open. For that matter, her heart might have actually completed a full somersault within the confines of her chest at the mere idea.

It couldn't be true.

Not when she had five hundred other things to obsess about this afternoon.

She blinked the cartoon hearts out of her eyes and managed to swallow the rest of her cracker. "What about living life on our own terms? What about no more constantly bending to suit the men in our lives?"

Giselle nudged her inside the suite and cranked the door open all the way to give them visibility out into the hallway. "We meant no bending over backwards to suit a man. But a little compromise is a healthy thing. Do you really feel like Jackson wants you to bend over backwards for him?"

Okay, so maybe she had a one-track mind, but Giselle's words brought to mind all sorts of erotic bending-over images. She could hardly stand to be in the bordello room these days without getting all hot and bothered over memories of what she and Jackson had shared in here. "Um. Not in the sense that you mean, I guess."

Giselle held up both hands. "I'm not touching that one. I just meant to say that it's okay to fall for a great guy." She withdrew a compact from her purse and handed it to Summer. "You should powder while we're talking. They'll be here any minute."

Summer had visions of appearing in a national magazine with a shiny face and started primping. No wonder Jackson liked starchy shirts. It definitely paid to be prepared. "Thank you."

Whipping a comb from the same bottomless purse, Giselle combed a few of Summer's many stray strands into place while she glared at her in the gilt-framed mirror hanging above the sitting area. "Back to my point, you don't want to walk away from big-time happiness just because the man didn't show up looking quite the way you expected. You could both compromise a little to find a middle ground, couldn't you?"

"It's not just that." She didn't need to wear sunglasses during interviews or do her errands wearing a spiked collar or anything. It wouldn't kill her to tone down on occasion. She was cool with that. "I can make a few concessions, but I'm not so sure he can. For that matter, I'm not sure he wants to take on me and all my public image problems. His life is a lot more complicated than I realized."

Although his goals were noble—a cleaner beach, protected coastline, a few breaks for small-time merchants to carve out a living among the heavy hitters in the resort industry. She had to give him credit for finding ways to strike a happy balance.

Damn it, if he was so good at finding his political balance in a cutthroat election, why couldn't he have figured out a relationship balance to make them both happy?

Then again, she had to ask herself, why hadn't she tried a little harder? She'd panicked at the first sign of trouble.

After a quick blast of hairspray to glue Summer's neatly combed hair in place, Giselle strode over to peer out the door and down the hall. "All I'm saying is that maybe you shouldn't be so quick to run. Just because you're still in the same state with the man doesn't change the fact that you peeled rubber out of that relationship."

And gave up.

Summer knew damn well she had given up too fast. But it had hurt to hear Jackson pushing her for more, nudging her closer to a commitment that scared her more than this interview.

"They're here!" Giselle flashed her a big, excited smile from the doorway, eyes alight with hope at what the magazine spread could mean for the business.

Summer's belly rumbled in nervous protest.

Had Jackson scared her as much as this? Maybe the two were a close tie.

She edged closer to the door and saw a new troop of camera-carrying strangers charging down the hallway. She vise-locked Giselle's wrist with a not-so-subtle plea to stay.

"If you help me make it through this, Giselle," she hissed through clenched teeth, hoping she'd be able to talk through her pasted-on smile when the reporters reached the door, "I promise I'll seriously consider planting my wandering feet here forever."

"Honey if you make it through this, you won't have to. If you get an endorsement as a decorator from the nation's biggest travel publication, the world will be your oyster." Giselle slid a wistful look in Summer's direction. "You'll just have to figure out where you want to go next."

JACKSON WANTED out of here.

Normally, he would have relished the opportunity to address a group of college kids full of fresh ideas and big dreams. But as he waited in a faculty lounge behind a large auditorium on the University of Miami campus for his speech to commence, all he could think about was Summer's big press conference today.

He should be *there*. With her.

Lucky shifted restlessly in the rolling office chair at a small conference table beside him. "One of the local cable stations will probably be down at Club Paradise this morning." He rolled his chair down a few feet and snagged a remote control from the head of the table. "Why don't you see if you can find her on TV instead of sitting here pretending you're rehearsing your speech?"

Jackson didn't waste any time pushing the necessary buttons. "How the hell would *you*, of all people, know what I'm pretending?"

"I think I'm offended." Lucky yanked the financial section of the paper from his briefcase and started to scan the contents. "Try channel nine."

"Excuse me if you don't strike me as Joe Perceptive.'' Jackson flipped the channel and waited for the picture to come up. And promptly sucked in a breath.

There she was.

Five minutes before he was supposed to take the podium and his concentration fractured at the sight of Summer conversing with an elegant woman in a light-blue pantsuit and carefully pinned caramel-colored hair. She looked sleek and New York all the way, while Summer looked…

Damn good.

She hadn't tried to thumb her nose at convention by wearing pink denim or flashy crystals. She'd unearthed a flowing, *subtle* floral dress that hinted at her eccentric nature without overstating the case. She'd even donned a strand of white beads that could almost be mistaken for pearls at first glance, but Jackson's careful inspection of the image on television assured him she actually wore little white moonstones in alternating shapes of stars and moons.

A grin twitched his lips.

Lucky dropped his paper to stare up at the screen. ''Looks like they've got her over a barrel.''

Jackson blinked, his narrowed gaze panning out from the close focus on Summer to take in the rest of the scene. ''What do you mean?''

Standing, Lucky brought his media-interpretation skills closer to the screen. ''See the women in the background straightening the flower vase and picking up something off the floor?''

Sure enough, when Jackson tore his gaze from Summer, he began to absorb the strange elements in the picture. Summer and her elegant guest both darting glances toward the hubbub behind them, an occasional elbow from off-camera sliding into view, a hum of white noise beneath the women's voices on the audio. "You think she's having trouble?"

"I think the local press corps caught her unaware by wanting to sit in on her moment in the spotlight. If she doesn't have any professional media handlers on staff, managing that kind of attention can be overwhelming for a novice."

His chest tightening with empathy, Jackson's gaze streaked back to Summer's delicate features. Only now did he notice the small worry lines above her brow, the stiff way she held her normally fluid, graceful body.

"You're a media handler." Jackson spoke the words aloud before a plan fully formed in his mind. A first for him, but if he ever succeeded in winning Summer back into his life, he had the feeling it wouldn't be the last time.

Lucky nodded. "One of my many talents."

"You could pry the wolves off her back long enough for her to finish up her work with the magazine, couldn't you?"

"You're asking *me* to ride in on the white horse and save *your* woman?"

Jesus, what was he thinking? Lucky hadn't won his moniker for his high percentage of winning election campaigns. Jackson would have to be an idiot to send in a smooth-talking pretty boy to save the day. "Of course not. It just occurred to me that if you can do it, I sure as hell ought to be able to manage it."

Lucky scrubbed his temples with his fingers. "I'm sure you could. Too bad you have a speech to make in two minutes."

Jackson's heart picked up rhythm as the whys and wherefores of a plan fell into place. "On the contrary, fortunately for me, one of your many talents is also crowd control."

Lucky's hands went up in defense position. "No way, Jack. You're not leaving me here—"

Unfazed, Jackson tugged his car keys out of his pocket and backed toward the side exit. "I'm trusting you to put a hell of a spin on my excuse so no one gets their feathers ruffled today. I need to hunt down a white charger and go kick some media butt to save the day."

"Damn it, Jackson, you'll be hanging yourself if you blow off another speech," Lucky called, chasing him into the university corridor.

"I've got it," Jackson shouted back as he skidded toward the second set of doors leading out of the building. "You can put a romance twist on it—Politician Forsakes Public Opinion to Win Back Muse."

Confident Lucky would figure out something despite the blistering string of curses he hurled across the campus lawns, Jackson sprinted to his car, praying that this time he'd figured out the right mix of strategy and impulsiveness to win back the woman he…

His fingers fumbled the keys as he tried to unlock the door because the first word that came to mind was *loved*.

Bending to retrieve the keys, he searched his brain for an alternative and found he didn't want one.

He loved Summer Farnsworth, damn it, and he couldn't wait to plead his case and tell her just how much.

# 16

*Keep in mind that the best quests last a lifetime...*

AFTER TALKING at length with the very patient *Wanderlust* reporter amid much interruption from the local press, Summer winced as the snap-happy brunette from the local arts weekly—Sheena something or other—bumped into Giselle's perfectly arranged rolling cart full of hors d'oeuvres. Stacks of crackers from the cheese board tumbled into the veggie tray.

*Calgon, take me away.*

Closing her eyes for a moment to mentally ground and center, Summer wished she hadn't bothered to look like Miss Mainstream U.S.A. today and had loaded up on the soothing energy of pink rose quartz crystals. The stress of juggling the various media camps was wearing away at her every last nerve. And it didn't help that two of the local reporters sported campaign buttons with Jackson's yin and yang symbol along with one of the slogans she'd helped craft.

She'd seen the reminders of her time with Jackson everywhere this week. Which of course, spurred reminders of the most private place Jackson carried that yin-yang symbol, followed by memories of what he looked like naked...

"Shall we get started on the photos then?" Madison

Blair, the reporter from *Wanderlust* magazine inquired, effectively interrupting Summer's inappropri-
ate reverie.

Oh sure. Why not snap a few in the Harem Suite
where someone from the local media had already
spilled a glass of red wine on the carpet? Her itinerary
could no longer be trusted now that some of the rooms
had been trampled in the local reporters' haste to get
first dibs on photographs. "That would be lovely. Let
me just check with my on-site staff to see which room
is ready first."

Whipping out her cell phone, Summer accidentally
jammed her previously hammered forefinger into the
number pad as she dialed Lainie. Pain throbbed
through her in time to mild mortification at the upshot
of a day that should have been flawless.

And better planned.

Madison waved off her concern. "That's quite all
right. We have a few other appointments around town
slotted for today so we need to keep a rather tight
schedule." She withdrew the copy of the itinerary
Summer had naively handed her when she first arrived.
"I'll just follow the list and we'll be out of your hair
in no time."

Nooo. Oh no. Summer was forced to hang up in
Lainie's ear to slow down the progress of her hard-
charging travel journalist guest.

Could the day turn anymore disastrous? For the
umpteenth time, she wished she possessed some of
Jackson's ability to smooth over rough patches with
his charm and natural sense of authority. Or maybe it
was simply his magnetic blue eyes and granite jaw that

distracted audiences and hypnotized them into following him.

Either way, she'd give her eyeteeth to boot out the members of the regional press who were continually hampering her day with Madison Blair and *Wanderlust*. "Um. Actually, it's been brought to my attention that a few of the rooms are a little—"

Madison paused, eyeing Summer expectantly.

Summer swallowed, scanned her memory banks for the right words that didn't convey "trashed" or "complete disarray" and came up empty.

A buzz among the milling local photographers averted her attention long enough to see what new crisis was in store. The buzz turned into discernible bits of conversation laced with the name *Jackson Taggart* just in time for her to glimpse a head of cropped sandy hair jogging into the midst of the small crowd.

Her heart stilled in her chest, then picked up a fast, erratic rhythm. "Ohmigod."

The *Wanderlust* writer stepped backward down the hall. "If that's all, Summer, we really do need to begin—"

She jumped into action, her ear still straining for whatever might be transpiring between Jackson and the other reporters. "Let me at least show you to the next suite." Which she sincerely hoped was adequately prepared. "Just take the elevator…here, follow me."

As she walked Madison to the elevator bank, they passed the throng around Jackson. From the middle of the crowd, she could hear his voice. "…so I'm here to see if I can win Summer back by doing her a big favor and prying the Miami media off her shoulders for an hour.''

Her heart melted.

Did he truly want to win her back? Moreover, had he really just implied he was here on a rescue mission? Independent woman of the world though she might be, she'd take any help she could get today.

''Shouldn't you be at the University of Miami campus today, Jackson?'' called one of the reporters.

She turned to glance at Madison, but the woman seemed as engrossed in the new arrival as she herself was. No surprise there. A woman would have to be devoid of a pulse not to notice the ambitious attorney.

From across the throng, snap-happy Sheena chimed in. ''Does Summer know you're trying to win her back?''

A few heads turned her in her direction, Madison's included. Summer couldn't help but smile even though she had no idea if she and Jackson stood a chance at making it work were they to try again.

From the agreeable flood of warmth and hope through her veins, it seemed her wary heart would be willing to try.

''Is that your sweetheart?'' Madison asked as they stood at the fringes of the gathering. The travel writer seemed less in a hurry now as she craned her neck to get a glimpse of the magnetic man attracting everyone's attention in the wide corridor outside the bordello suite.

Not sure how to answer, Summer couldn't help but smile as she offered up as much as she knew right now. ''He's a local politician I've had my eye on.''

She might have felt more possessive as elegant, sophisticated Madison lingered to stare, but the woman sported a diamond that could probably serve double duty as a doorknob. "I'd snap him up quick if I were you. It's not every day a woman finds a man willing to go out on a limb for her."

Summer felt an instant connection with Madison that an hour of discussion about decorating hadn't managed to elicit. Funny how talk of men had the power to bond females in a nanosecond.

She might have embarrassed herself by launching into a discussion of her feelings for Jackson if the elevator bell hadn't rung just then.

Lainie stepped through the doors the moment they parted, high color in her cheeks and her normally perfect hair only slightly askew. She clutched a sheaf of crisp white papers in one hand and pulled one from the stack to hand to Madison. "I think you'll find this schedule better suited to your needs today, Ms. Blair. The luxurious harem suite that Summer has designed is on the fourth floor."

The wine-soaked harem suite?

Madison backed into the elevator with her camera crew, flipping a strand of caramel-colored hair out of one eye as her eyes sped over the new schedule. "Thank you. We really do need to get in gear so we can hit some other sites today. We should have something on you in the magazine after the holidays."

The elevator doors were sliding closed as Summer called to her. "I'll be up to check on you in a little bit!" Turning to Lainie she frowned. "The harem suite? What about the wine?"

Lainie looped an arm around Summer's shoulders. "Brianne had some handheld cleaner gadget that sucked it right out of the carpet. You'd never know it was there. Giselle went to get some G-rated cookies to pass out to Jackson's audience and I've got house-keeping tweaking details in the last few rooms on Madison's list. Everything will be back in order in no time."

They stood in the wide corridor that was slowly clearing out, thanks to Jackson redirecting the local media into one of the small lounge areas overlooking the ocean. Summer's feet automatically followed the sound of his voice.

"Can you believe he showed up here today?" She scarcely believed it herself.

Hadn't she walked out on him when he'd tried to pin her down? They hadn't spoken all week and yet here he was just when she needed him most. Just when her heart had realized she'd been too scared to be honest with him when he'd pressed her for commitment.

"Of course I believe it. Any dolt can see the man's crazy about you." Lainie paused as they reached the archway into the small lounge where Jackson was speaking.

Giselle had beaten them there, already circulating food at the back of the room. Coffee was being rolled in to sit beside trays piled high with sweets. She toasted Summer with a glass of water as she spoke with one of the wait staff.

Tears sprang to Summer's eyes as she realized they were pulling it off. She, Giselle, Lainie and Brianne were actually going to make something spectacular of this crazy couples resort they'd inherited. Maybe not tomorrow and maybe not next week, but they had the skills to make Club Paradise a fantastic vacation destination, a memorable resort for every guest and for that matter, they could make it damn profitable.

Pride filled her as she watched Jackson patiently answer questions about state education reform, pride for her own accomplishments and his. The man who'd hidden her away on his boat for their first date was not the same man who'd claimed her in front of a room full of reporters today. He was proud of her, too—quirky past and all—and he hadn't been afraid to let the world know it today.

Brianne appeared on her other side to flash her a thumbs-up sign. Apparently the rest of the room clean-up was on target and running smoothly. She nudged Summer with an elbow and leaned closer to whisper. "You know, the sooner you tie things up with Madison upstairs, the sooner you'll be able to tackle that sexy politician giving you the eye."

Summer smiled as—sure enough—Jackson's gaze met hers above the crowd seated in wingbacks and taking notes. Lingered.

Her heart did the somersault thing again, making her feel lightheaded. Good God, she was practically giddy.

"You're right," Summer whispered back, doing her best to ignore the butterflies flitting around in her belly. "If you happen to be around when he finishes up, would you tell him I'll meet him down by the water?"

"I have the feeling he'd track you down wherever you are, but I'll let him know."

Summer tore herself away from watching Jackson, content in the knowledge they'd talk later. And maybe, if he was willing to compromise a little and so was she, they could find that balance that had been missing from their relationship.

As she headed for the elevator bank to oversee the rest of the *Wanderlust* photo shoot, she could hear one of the reporter's questions from the lounge.

"So how do you see a notorious club diva fitting into your high-visibility lifestyle, Mr. Taggart?"

Although the elevator opened in front of her, Summer strained to hear the answer to the question.

Jackson's voice rumbled through the hallways and right into her heart.

"Just perfectly."

JACKSON SPOTTED her standing at the edge of the surf at sunset. She'd tied the hem of her flowing floral dress into a knot at her knees to keep the garment out of the water. Sandals discarded on the sand, she traced pictures in the wet mud with her toe in between the encroaching waves.

His heart caught in his chest at the thought of being close to her again. The week without her had been more painful than he could have imagined. She'd become so important, so fast.

He'd left his jacket and tie in Brianne's office, his shoes and socks on the deck behind the club. Maybe a part of him wanted to show her he knew how to loosen up. Mostly he wanted to shed every piece of clothing he wore and wrap her in his arms. Lie her down and make slow, sweet love to her until they were both delirious, mindless for one another.

She spied him then, lifting a hand to shade her eyes against the falling sun. Even without her pink braids, her blond hair took on a rosy hue in the fiery last threads of daylight.

"You saved me today." Her words floated on the breeze as he closed the distance between them. "I don't know how I would have handled the crowd if you hadn't shown up to help me."

Damn but it felt good to have her look at him that way. Grateful. Hungry. And not wary anymore.

"Looked like you were managing okay to me." He stopped short of touching her, jamming his hands in his pockets to curb the urge. He'd messed up before by rushing her, pushing for what he wanted instead of listening to what she might need.

"How did you know I was in trouble?" She took a step into the water and skimmed a toe across the surface to send a ripple up over his feet.

Not a problem. He simply rolled up the cuffs of his trousers, undeterred. "Lucky had a sense that the local newshounds would show up for your event. I didn't think to ask him about it, but I'd be willing to bet he couldn't get all the coverage for my speech today because half the Miami correspondents were making plans to be here instead." His manager might occasionally annoy the hell out of him, but Jackson had to hand it to the guy—he knew his business. "Anyway, I clicked on the TV and there you were."

"You saw me falling flat on my face and decided to lend a hand?"

"Hell no. Mostly I was just getting a kick out of seeing you in conservative clothes until Lucky cued me in to some of the background details. I wouldn't have had a clue you were surrounded by interlopers without his help." He reached out a hand to her, hoping he had the timing right now. "And yeah, when I saw a chance to let you know publicly that I wasn't giving up easily, I practically flew here to jump on the opportunity."

She slid her fingers to rest inside his palm, her skin smooth and cool against the heat of his. "Won't you be lambasted for running out on your university speech today?" Smiling, she tugged a wind-whipped strand of long hair out from under her chin. "Not that I've been keeping tabs on your daily schedule or anything."

"I rescheduled for tomorrow and I promised to unveil my ideas for state education reform while I'm there, so all has been forgiven." Thanks to Lucky's damage control crisis had been averted on that front. Now it was up to Jackson to heal the rift with Summer, to show her he was willing to wait for her. "Assuming I don't fall flat on *my* face, that is."

"Not a chance." She tugged him deeper into the water so that the shallow waves rolled over their ankles. "You helped me by creating a diversion so I could finish up my interview with *Wanderlust,* and now I owe you one. Want me to create a diversion for you tomorrow? I bought this amazing silver toga that would be just the thing."

"You can show up any way you want, Summer. I'll be glad to take you however I can have you."

Summer stared into those earnest blue eyes until she practically drowned in them. She believed him. He didn't care about the crystals or the clothes, the club madam job she took upon herself at the Moulin Rouge Lounge or her penchant for public displays of affection.

He only wanted *her.*

"What about the whole commitment factor? I know you're more ready to move forward than I am, but I—"

"You're right. I'm ready for you now, but I've realized that doesn't mean I can coerce you into more commitment than you're ready for." He drew her closer, his broad, warm hands steadying her hips, stabilizing her world. "I just hope that some day…"

He cut himself off as if he didn't want to pressure her. But after today, Summer was thinking maybe a little persuasion in that department would be welcome. She'd been ducking and running for far too long.

"I think there's a very good chance that some day I could be swayed to your way of thinking." She waited for him to realize what she was saying, noted the way the shades of blue shifted and lightened in his eyes. She rushed on, not ready to fully examine that fragile new desire inside her yet. But soon… "I've already committed myself to South Beach."

"You're kidding." As if sensing her mood, he smiled, traced the trail of buttons up her dress with one finger. "You mean to tell me the gypsy is going to grow roots?"

She smiled, warming to the idea of commitments to men and places. Ties to a community and gentle ties around her heart. "As long as you spirit me away to somewhere exotic for a vacation every now and then, I'm never going to move away from South Beach."

As if seeing his opening, Jackson the ever-observant attorney narrowed in on the opportunity. "Are you saying you'll go on vacation with me, Summer?"

"I'm actually…" She paused for dramatic effect. "…very *committed* to the idea. What do you think?"

"Come away with me after the election is over. Win or lose, I'll have some time to myself this fall. We can go wherever you want." His hands spread out along her collarbone, smoothed over her shoulders. "Head down to the Florida Keys. Wing over to Paris for a few days. You name it."

"How do you feel about South Dakota? There's this school I want to revisit to see how the latest squad of cheerleaders are doing." She'd been thinking about the way she'd run from her ties there. Maybe she'd feel all the more ready to dig into her new home if she had some closure on her past. "I seem to remember there's a biker fest in Sturgis every year. You can see if Aidan wants to fire up his hog so he and Brianne can join us for a few days."

"Perfect. I'll take a picture of you in front of Mt. Rushmore in your silver toga. We can e-mail it to the South Beach paper so you can make headlines from afar."

Warmth spiraled through her, inside and out. He really was as crazy as her. He simply planned his moments of unconventional defiance a little better than she did.

"You sure you don't mean so *you* can make headlines from afar? I think I've got your number, Mr. Future Legislator." Her feet were already digging into the shifting sands, rooting her to South Beach and planting her firmly beside Jackson.

"You don't know the half of it." He pulled her into his arms, tucking her body against his chest while he drew his hand through the wind-tangled mass of her hair. "Not only am I going to ride your coattails onto the social pages, I'm also naming you my official muse when it comes to politics. I didn't have one good idea all last week while we were apart and then today, flying over here to try and win you back, I had this massive brainstorm for education reform."

"Oh really? Have you considered maybe you're only using me for your own personal gain?" She wriggled even closer to him, cementing their hips together in a message he couldn't ignore.

A rough growl rumbled through his throat. "I won't lie. I'm gaining a hell of a lot by being with you." He bent closer to whisper in her ear. "But I'd like to think I bring a few things to the mix, too."

"Is that right?" The warmth inside her turned to scorching heat at the sexy stereo sound of his smooth baritone.

"Oh yeah. Come back to the hotel with me and I'll remind you of just a few of the fringe benefits you'll be receiving."

Her heart slugged so hard against his chest he had to feel the heavy beat. "I think I remember them. Well."

"But you don't know this one." He leaned back just a fraction, tipped her chin up to meet his gaze. "I love you, Summer."

Joy tripped through her along with happy, positive vibes that no amount of rose quartz crystals could have ever generated.

The truth that she'd been stowing away inside her since the press conference bubbled at her lips.

"It just so happens I realized today that I love you, too." Thank God her friends had given her the shove she'd needed to get her head together, to help her see what was right in front of her.

"Only today?" He smiled, bent closer to graze his lips over her mouth.

"Right about the time you sailed into Club Paradise to give me the hand I never would have asked for." She nibbled his lower lip, thinking about what he'd just said. "You mean you knew before today?"

"Are you kidding? I'm the man who knows what he wants and goes after it. It might have taken me a while to admit it to myself, but I knew the moment I set eyes on these lips in the Moulin Rouge Lounge."

A wildly romantic notion coming from such a practical man. Summer couldn't help but smile. "No one can predict true love on the basis of a mouth."

"Ah, you underestimate how much thought I put into the matter. How much strategy I employed to weed out all the wrong women." He dragged kisses along her jaw to nip at her ear. "Besides, you read the future in people's palms. Who's to say I couldn't see my future in this perfect mouth of yours?"

She licked her lips and thrilled at the way his gaze zeroed in on the movement. She sensed a wealth of untapped power here.

"You haven't seen anything yet. If you think these lips are hot now, you ought to see what they can do with a little encouragement."

She pulled her feet out of the sand and edged closer to the shore. And the hotel. And the bed that awaited them.

Jackson had her hauled up in his arms before she could even think about making her own way back.

And judging by his low growl of approval, she had

the feeling she'd have to write off her beach-bound sandals to the incoming tide. If her luck held, it would be many long, delicious hours before she could possibly retrieve them.

**SINGLE IN SOUTH BEACH**
*continues!*
*Don't miss Renzo Cesare's story*
*ONE NAUGHTY NIGHT,*
*Temptation 951, coming in November 2003*

*Turn the page for a sneak peek*
*of Renzo's tale....*

# 1

RENZO CESARE HAD KISSED plenty of women in his day.

Not that he considered himself a connoisseur or anything, because that just sounded plain sleazy. But he had some experience to compare Esme Giles's kiss against, and that tentative brush of her soft pink mouth over his completely obliterated all memory of holding anyone else in his arms.

He'd told himself he would let her set the pace tonight since he'd intercepted her from meeting her real date in the first place. According to his sister, no woman wanted to be insulated from life by a hulking Cesare who would claim mob affiliation in a heartbeat if it would scare potential predators.

Yet here he was, doing his gentlemanly best to save Esme Giles from herself and all the while falling under the spell of her sweet pink lips.

Lips he found himself parting with the sweep of his tongue. Damn. Damn. Damn. He hadn't meant to do that.

But man, she was sweet.

She tasted like rum and something more sugary. Sort of like the strawberry lip-gloss girls in his junior high used to wear. All innocence. How had he gone his whole life without realizing strawberry lip-gloss still turned him on nearly twenty years later?

Her body sank into his a little more, giving him all the more appreciation for the shape and feel of her bare breasts beneath her dress.

Goodbye all innocence. Hello sensual woman.

The hard beads of her nipples had his body answering hers in kind, encouraging him to do all the things to her they both wanted so badly....

Except they were in the middle of a goddamn dance floor.

Renzo broke their kiss, unable to pull away from her totally without disrupting her balance. Besides, he didn't dare move away from her quickly or he'd end up exposing them both a bit too...intimately.

Esme's eyes remained closed a moment, and when she lifted her lids to gaze up at him again, the passion-clouded expression he saw there made him want to drag her somewhere private and—

Wait.

Wasn't he supposedly saving her from that kind of fate when he'd told her a whopper of a fib tonight?

Backing them off the side of the floor, Renzo peeled himself away from her with more than a little regret.

"Maybe you ought to walk me up to my room now," she whispered, her voice barely audible above the synthesized whine of the next dance song.

"Good idea." Renzo steered her through the crowd, using his body as a shield for her to make sure no drunken idiots copped a feel on the way.

He could not, should not, would not, get anymore involved with Esme. The whole charade had been ill-conceived and it would be least embarrassing for all parties if he simply said good-night to her right now.

Just as soon as he knew she was safely inside her room.

Once they cleared the Moulin Rouge Lounge and hit the bank of elevators, she paused, fishing in her purse.

"I'm on the fourth floor in the Sensualist's Suite. Maybe I'd better find my key." She shook her purse as the elevator arrived. Apparently convinced the key lay within the white satin bag, Esme began the search with determination etched on her delicate jawline.

"The Sensualist's Suite?" He had no idea why he tortured himself by asking as they stepped inside the elevator.

Maybe because liars deserved to be tortured.

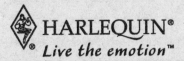

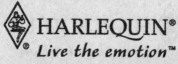

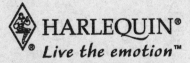

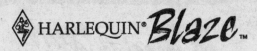

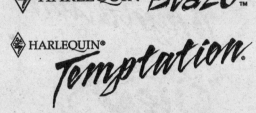

# HARLEQUIN®

# Blaze™

## COMING NEXT MONTH

### #109 FLAVOR OF THE MONTH Tori Carrington
*Kiss & Tell, Bk. 2*

*Four friends. Countless secrets...* Pastry shop owner Reilly Cudowski
has spent most of her life squelching her secret cravings. But when delicious
Benjamin Kane shows up, she can't help indulging a little.
Only, the more she has Ben, the more she wants. So what else can
Reilly do but convince him that a lifetime of desserts can be even sweet-
er...?

### #110 OVER THE EDGE Jeanie London

After ten years of patient planning, Mallory Hunt finally has Jake Trinity
right where she wants him. He's contracted her security expertise, and
while she's at it, she'll push *his* sensual edges. Their long-ago first meeting—
and its steamy kiss—changed her life, and now it's time
for payback. But Mallory doesn't count on the intense heat between
them or the fact she doesn't *want* this to end!

### #111 YOURS TO SEDUCE Karen Anders
*Women Who Dare, Bk. 2*

When firefighter Lana Dempsey finally tackles fellow firefighter
Sean O'Neill in the...showers, it's a five-alarm blaze. Stripped of their uni-
forms, it's what Lana's always wanted. Having had a crush on Sean since
forever, she'd never been brave enough to do anything about it. Until the
bet she'd made with her girlfriends gives her the courage
to finally squelch that burning desire for Sean!

### #112 ANYTHING GOES... Debbi Rawlins

Seven days of sun, sand and sex, sex, sex! That's exactly what
Carly Saunders needs—anonymous sex...and lots of it. She has
one week of sin before she heads home to a teaching job—and her
place as the pastor's daughter. So she's going to make this week count.
Only, she never dreams she'll meet Rick, her best friend growing up.
Or that he'll have the same agenda...

Visit us at www.eHarlequin.com

HBCNM1003